BOOKS BY LAURA (L.A.)MARIANI

Angels & Demons

The Fallen Angel

The Hot Ghost

The Bad Saint

The Fallen Hero

The Hot Priest

The Bad Santa

Box Set

Angels & Demons

Untamed Hearts

The BAD Boy

The BAD Girl

Holiday Romance

14 Days to Love Series: Short Sweet Steamy

Parisian Serendipity

Venetian Whispers

Mumbay Surprise

Romeo in Rome

New York Melody

Artic Embrace

Santorini Sunsets

Havana Heat

Barcelona Dreams

Marrakesh Magic

Vienna Waltz

Sydney Sparks

Amsterdam Affair

Cape Town Safari

Box Set

14 Days to Love: Short Sweet Steamy

Twelve Days of Christmas Series

A Partridge in a Pear Tree: Hot Spicy Christmas Novella

Two Turtle Doves: Hot Spicy Christmas Novella

Three French Hens: Hot Spicy Christmas Novella

Four Calling Birds: Hot Spicy Christmas Novella

Five Golden Rings: Hot Spicy Christmas Novella

Six Geese a-Laying: Hot Spicy Christmas Novella

Seven Swans a-Swimming: Hot Spicy Christmas Novella

Eight Maids a-Milking: Hot Spicy Christmas Novella

Nine Ladies Dancing: Hot Spicy Christmas Novella

Ten Lords a-Leaping: Hot Spicy Christmas Novella

Eleven Pipers Piping: Hot Spicy Christmas Novella

Twelve Drummers Drumming: Hot Spicy Christmas Novella

Box Set

Twelve Days of Christmas

Shadowbrook Paranormal Series

A Halloween Romance: Enchanted in Shadowbrook

The Midnight Hour:A Halloween Shadowbrook Romance

Navy Seals Hunks Series

SEALed Hearts

SEALed with a Kiss

SEALed Undercover

SEALed Pursuit

SEALed Love Code

SEALed beyond Duty

Box Set

Navy SEAL Hunks

A Royal Romance Trilogy

A Coronation Weekend Romance

The Wicked Princess

The Lost Kingdom

Box Set

A Royal Romance Trilogy

The Nine Lives of Gabrielle Series

Gabrielle (prequel/first in series)

Her Little Secret (series spin off)

For Three She Plays

A New York Adventure

Searching for Goren

Tasting Freedom

For Three She Strays

Paris Toujours Paris

Me Myself and Us

Freedom Over Me

For Three She Stays

London Calling

Back in Your Arms

The Greatest Love

Box Sets

For Three She Plays - Book 1-3

For Three She Strays - Book 4-6

For Three She Stays - Book 7-9

The Nine Lives of Gabrielle Book 1-9 + 3 Bonus stories

Box Set - Italian Edition

Le Nove Vite di Gabrielle: Libri 1-9 + 3 Bonus

Le Nove Vite di Gabrielle - Edizione Deluxe: Libri 1-9+3 Bonus & Spin Off (Il Suo Piccolo Segreto)

THE NINE LIVES OF GABRIELLE

DELUXE EDITION

LAURA (L.A.) MARIANI

THE
PEOPLE
ALCHEMIST

ISBN: 978-1-917104-35-7

CONTENTS

THE NINE LIVES OF GABRIELLE

PREFACE

The Nine Lives of Gabrielle is a whirlwind romance and a journey of self-discovery between three of the most beautiful cities in the world: London, New York and Paris.

Like the nine lives of cats, Gabrielle first plays, then strays, and finally, she wants to stay.

But is the course of true love always plain sailing? Sometimes not, and so you might need some more lives, right?

That's exactly what happened when I started writing Gabrielle; the story kept unfolding, more and more to say.

So I kept going.

And here it is, a contemporary city life romance to make you laugh (unless you have no sense of humour ;-)), reflect, gasp and perhaps shed a little tear while enjoying the excitement of the Big Apple, dreaming of Paris and longing for London.

And then I kept going some more with the spin off (well, Paola and Martin deserved more than just passages here and there).

I hope you'll enjoy reading it as much as I enjoyed writing it.

Laura xxx

INTRODUCTION

Self-Image is our self-limiting portable box.

Our world and everything in it reflects our mental attitude toward ourselves. We constantly adjust to its confines like thermostats, and when we step too far from our comfort zone, we return to familiar paradigms. Sometimes, in the pursuit of fulfilment, we betray not only others but also ourselves.

Self-Image is the ultimate internal regulator: whenever the temperature rises above our comfort level, it will take us back to the base like a thermostat. Self-image is determined by the paradigms that run our life and mind unconsciously.

Are you searching and never finding?

The perfect place, perfect man or woman, perfect career?

Do you know what you are looking for in the first place? Sometimes we even cross the line and our moral compass to meet our needs.

What if we are always choosing people who don't allow intimacy?

Is it because, deep down, we don't want intimacy? Or are we afraid we'd lose ourselves entirely if we let ourselves be loved?

Committed to not committing.

Creating what you want to have or achieve in the future implies that you understand the here and now.

Constantly chasing what you could have or whom you might meet means you ignore what exists all around you that already IS incredible. Or, even worse, the wonderful people who are all around you.

Worse still, unless we resolve our deep-rooted issues, address our core needs and then up-level our self-image, we will reach the "temperature" we are comfortable in sooner or later. Then Self-sabotage comes in.

And there we start again.

Happiness and fulfilment already exist in your life. It starts with you. First and foremost.

Enjoy your life as it comes whilst working to be the best you.

The rest will take care of itself.

Gabrielle is an excellent novel that is captivating, moving, and terrific all at the same time!

Gabrielle astounded me from start to finish with its captivating literature courtesy of the author Laura Mariani whose novel is full of phenomenal characterization and many moving elements laced throughout that will keep you on the edge of your seat.

I adore novels like this one that focus on a strong female narrative but some can be predictable and lackluster. However, as I got lost in Gabrielle I realized it is far from this.

Instead, it is a sensational, unique novel with many compelling elements laced throughout that no reader should miss.

— AIMEE , THE RED HEADED BOOK LOVER

I personally am not a reader, I prefer audiobooks for fiction stories.

With that said, Gabrielle was such an easy read, I quickly fell into the story and could not put the book down.

I read it all the way through and felt that I had formed a connection with Gabrielle and could relate to her journey of self discovery. There are tons of little nuggets throughout the book that really resonated with me that I intend to apply to my life moving forward.

It also lended another perspective on what it was like to go through quarantine as a single which I can now empathize with. Great story and great lessons!

I look forward to the next novel from Laura!

— STEVE BURN JR - HAPPY READER

THE NINE LIVES OF GABRIELLE

DELUXE EDITION

PROLOGUE

Time is passing by relentlessly. Time past, time present, time future.

But this primary fundamental of physical reality is not what it seems: it's an optical illusion.

Physicists tell us that things in the quantum world do not happen in linear steps. They happen now. But you are only aware of the reality you choose to observe.

Consciousness creates the material world—the linear passing of time in stark contrast with the seemingly random crossing of time in our consciousness.

A constant stream of consciousness.

. . .

Everything is NOW - the constant flow connected by some force within each person. And memories provide a continual connection to events, places and people.

There are infinite possibilities that the world can offer at every moment.

And just like that, one day, everything can change ...

"YOU'RE ONLY HERE NOW;
YOU'RE ONLY ALIVE IN THIS MOMENT"
- **JON KABAT-ZINN**

GABRIELLE

FROM THE DIARY OF

Your life can change at any point in time. You just need to decide who you want to be, what you want to do or have. And just like that, everything changes …

"I BLINKED MY EYES AND IN AN INSTANT,
DECADES HAD PASSED."
— JOHN MARK GREEN

GABRIELLE

G abrielle woke up, the overnight video still playing on her iPad.

"I am a Goddess, I am a Queen ... I am valued ... if I want it, I got it."
The rain was falling thick and fast. You could smell it in the air. Boy, it was noisy: the thunder, the rain ... It was so dark; winter was definitely coming.

"What day is it?" They all feel the same right now. Nowhere to go, nothing to do, nobody to see. Oh yes, it's Saturday. Who cares? Does it really make a difference?

"Keeping a routine gives me some parvence of normality, for myself really. Glowing up for myself, so to speak, self-discipline is self-love someone said.."

Yes, but sometimes though, it's such a drag...

. . .

The overnight video with looped affirmations was a bit of a thing to get used to: it kept waking her up during the night - maybe it was the screen's glare or subconscious resistance. However, she got used to it eventually and can now sleep for the entire night.

"This time is working for me ... re-wiring, reconstructing."

Gabrielle thought about how everything had changed one day, just like that.

It's amazing how life can turn just in a second. Uncontrollably. All the things you always wanted to do on pause. Until someone else decides to press the play button again.

It is easier to think that way somehow - an external force controlling your life, stopping you from achieving all the things you've always wanted to do, being the amazing being you always believed you were going to be. Funny.

Tomorrow, always longing for tomorrow, whereas everything in you ought to reject it. Then, suddenly, there almost wasn't a tomorrow.

To be fair, she enjoyed the alone time. She had always been a loner: as a child lost in her books, as an adult chasing the next win in the never-ending climb. She had cancelled many events before, dates, and meetings with friends at the last minute. There was always tomorrow. There was always something more important to do.

. . .

People were amazed by her unwavering confidence and strength; they looked up to her like some sort of Wonder Woman.

"Mirror, Mirror of them all, Who's the fairest of them all?"

Sometimes she just didn't feel too good about herself, and pretending was just too strenuous. It was exhausting and draining.

Now, there's no need to make up excuses.

Lockdown has been good for her, some time to focus on herself with little distraction. Getting to know who Gabrielle actually is or wants to be. Getting to like this Gabrielle, perhaps even love. And level up.

She looked out of the window onto Canonbury Square Gardens; the rain was coming down incessantly.

"I love this area of London. George Orwell lived in the square somewhere, I think", many significant figures from the arts and literary worlds have lived in the square. That was part of the appeal when she moved three years ago, the last move in the climb - the listed Georgian townhouse.

The outdoor seatings are engraved with the names of people who had lived in the square. A physical token or memories always present.

IN MEMORY OF EDDIE AND MABEL WALTERS WHO
LIVED IN CANONBURY SQUARE

. . .

On a *normal* Saturday, she would have popped in at The Estorick and looked at the latest exhibition, got lost in the surrounding, feasting her eyes, feeding the soul.

Perhaps bring her coffee in the Square Gardens; there are always people there.

The Friends of Canonbury Square volunteers do such a good job keeping the gardens so clean and neat.

"What time is it? Definitely coffee time. One needs coffee to meditate."

Gabrielle loved the smell of the coffee permeating the house, slowly but surely, a ripple effect, a sinuous wave propagating everywhere. Gabrielle made her bed first: someone somewhere said all successful entrepreneurs do so, the first task of the day-accomplished sort of thing. So much easier not to, but she did it anyway. Bed done. Coffee ready.

"Time for meditation now."

She had tried complete silence before but found that guided meditation was somehow easier. Someone, something to help with the ever-wondering thoughts going through her mind. But she found mantra meditation even better. The relentless repetition of the exact words has a reassuring, calming, almost numbing effect on her. Something to focus on for ten minutes or so.

"Getting good with these tapes," she reassured herself.

"I think I'll light up a candle to get me in the mood."

. . .

The flickering light in the dark room, thunder and the pitter platter of the rain against the window was playing in the background: she sat down, crossed-legged.

"Tell me again, why oh why do people sit down cross-legged to meditate?" She asked herself. She always got cramps. And always in the same foot, which then goes numb.
    She did it anyway. OK, here we go...

"Shreem Brzee, Shreem Brzee, Shreem, Brzee," Dr Pillai was chanting, and Gabrielle repeated along. Out loud.
    "108 times is a lot of times to repeat out loud."

Stop. Focus.

"Shreem Brzee, Shreem Brzee..." sip of coffee, "Shreem Brzee, Shreem Brzee..." rambles, rambles. Boom.

Bang! I think the neighbours are going for their daily walk, their door as loud as they are.
    "Shreem Brzee, Shreem Brzee"... My daily walk is out of the question for now.

She found peace of mind in walking – not a surprise there as she always really enjoyed it. The pandemic gave Gabrielle a new, more in-depth appreciation of being out there, alone, in gratitude for life. Appreciating everything that she's so lucky to be able to experience.

However, there was a limit: as much as she loved it, she didn't quite like getting soaked. People who golf don't seem to mind the rain.

"I'm not one of those," said Gabrielle. "I love being by the water, just not drenched in it."

She always loved the smell of water, such a sense of peace and tranquillity. She grew up by the water.

Angel Canal is a great place for long walks, she thought. The sunshine peeking through the clouds, the water moving with the breeze glistening like a dance.

"Shreem Brzee ... Shreem Brzee."

At the weekend, it's usually hustle and bustle, full of city professionals sipping their dairy-free latte whilst sending the last email before enjoying the weekend.

Not now.

Now she has the canal almost to herself. It was odd. The water moving steadily continuously, rocking the boats like a lullaby, the sun capturing the movements.

"Isn't it wonderful?"

The boats look restless, and so does she.

C-O-N-C-E-N-T-R-A-T-E.

. . .

"Shreem Brzee, Shreem Brzee ... Shreem Brzee. "

"How long is left now," Gabrielle peaked at the YouTube video playing, "another few minutes. Never realised ten minutes is such a long time."

Concentrate Gabri.

"Shreem Brzee ... Shreem Brzee", 107, "Shreem Brzee."
    Namaste, meditation done.

Damn, the coffee is cold now. I'll make another before I start with my morning pages. Gabrielle began free-writing journaling at the beginning of the first lockdown. The outpouring of unrestrained consciousness on a page, unbridled confessions or, better still, therapy, but free. Julia says it should be done first thing in the morning, without fail, before the conscious mind takes over, AND for at least three pages.

Some days, it was difficult enough to write even one. Some days, Gabrielle could write forever. She was never one to keep a diary. But this, she learned to enjoy, eventually, and stuck with it. It's amazing what comes up sometimes when you start writing.

BY HAND.

The movement of the pen along the paper, accompanying the free stream of uncensored thoughts, is therapy in itself. Gabrielle wasn't used to writing by hand anymore. Her handwriting was illegible sometimes. Heck, not great grammar either; there is no auto-correct spelling. But that is the point of morning pages: to free the mind up from the ever-present Inner Critic and let it flow. The future becomes the present, becomes the past, and becomes the present.

"Who writes by hand anymore?" she thought, holding the hot steaming bowl.

Gabrielle sat in the small alcove by the window, looking at the rain falling down, fresh coffee on the side table, notebook on her lap and started writing.

DEAR DIARY,
Why, oh why, did I write that? It feels like being a teenager again, even worse, being back at school. Yuck, couldn't have picked a worst time. So much of it, thankfully, is a blur - a purposeful blur, a closed door behind, never to be reopened.
Why is it coming up now? Go away. GO AWAY.

But the pen kept going, unwavering ... And so Gabrielle kept writing ...

Why are girls always so mean? To other girls, I mean.

"Gabri, why don't you go and mix with the other girls?" the teacher was trying to move her along as she talked to *maman*.
"Gabrielle is not mixing very well, Mrs Arkin. Don't get me

wrong, her grades are excellent; it's the social interactions that are lacking."

Mean, mean, mean. Secondary school - a random assembly of hormonal humans trying to assert their identity - is a recipe for disaster. Give me a book and paintbrushes anytime; they beat people 100 to 1.

Ugh. Secondary school and living in a small village. The quintessential village with thousand Hyacinths Bucket, pardon Bouquet.

A deadly combination.

> NOTHING GOOD COMES OUT OF VILLAGES EITHER,
> IT IS ALWAYS THE SAME THING:
> "*BLACKMAIL, SEXUAL DEVIANCE, SUICIDE, AND MURDER*" -
> INSPECTOR BARNABY.

"Gabri, why are you dressed like that? Gabri, what would Mrs So and So think,
  Gabri, you can't do that, Gabri. Are you listening?"

"You need to look your best, Gabri; it is better to be envied than pitied."

. . .

There must be more to life than this. She wanted to show them all.

"I'm strong and smart, I don't need anybody, and I can do it. I'll show them", she kept repeating to herself.

The pint-size village made her feel even smaller, the beach and the coastline the only relief. Ah, she loved being by the sea; she could sit pondering for hours.

So free, so calm, majestic and devastatingly strong. Full of hidden treasures.

She wanted to be like the ocean. Free and majestic, strong.

Free. Climbing the corporate ladder. Strong. She always aspired to a career at the top, no matter what, no matter where being the best. Rich and successful, of course.

One day she knew she was going to be.

Gabrielle had wanted to escape as fast as she could. She always knew she wanted to leave. Escape from Alcatraz, or at least that's how it felt.

And she did.

"Gabri, you are going to be alone in London. What happens if you are sick? What if you can't find a job?" her mother was having a fit.

"I'll survive, ma."

. . .

"You can always come back home, you know."
She was determined not to. Failure was never an option.

As she was boarding the train to London with all her belongings crammed in a couple of suitcases, she knew it was the right decision. Her parents had come to say goodbye, her mother crying, of course.
The dispatcher blew the whistle; it was time to go.
One last hug.

The train started moving faster and faster and faster. The village quickly fading behind her, and she felt the invisible shackles loosening. Slowly. She felt lighter. Her nose was pressed against the cold window, soaking every bit of the new views.

Arriving in London was like shredding too tight-fitting skin. Just like that, everything changed - she was now wearing a new one.
Nobody really cares or knows who you are and what you do here. That's part of its appeal: the beauty of living in total solitude and anonymity amongst millions of people.

A few hours' journey but a million miles apart.

"Funny," she thought.
"Victoria Station", announced the conductor.

Gabrielle looked at her belongings: she packed light, minimal luggage to start afresh. The heavier baggage was yet to be evident to her.

. . .

She stepped into the platform, her feet firmly on the ground.

The main roof of Victoria station glinting in the lunchtime sun, its slopes covering an area equivalent to three football pitches. It was one o'clock, and the station was jammed packed with people zig-zagging each other.

"Hey, lady, watch where you are going!"

"Sorry," she responded. Gabrielle joined the long queue in the black taxi rack outside the station.
"Hello, love."

"Camden Passage, Islington, please," Gabrielle said to the taxi driver.
Here we go.

Her first *bijou* apartment in London, estate agents speak for a studio flat where you can't even swing a cat. She loved it. It was just above Decadent Vintage, one of the many shops in the passage. She bought her first vintage Dior there.

In the first months when she first moved in, she sat for hours by the window watching the world go by: the weekend bargain hunters, the antique market, the hustle and bustle of restaurants, cafes and market stalls. The outsider looking in.

. . .

She loved browsing through fashionable contemporary clothing, modern designer jewellery, Japanese art prints, and specialist antique, silverware, and vintage clothing. The retro shops provided the backdrop for market stalls selling affordable collectables, vintage clothes and *objets d'art* that find their way into antique shops and homes all over the world. What's not to love?

She even loved the daily noise coming out of the Camden Head and its free comedy club, seven nights a week.

Gabrielle still enjoys the occasional shopping spree there: some British and international artisan cheeses at Pistachio & Pickle Dairy and the artisanal chocolates at Paul A. Young.

"I wonder when the shops will open again," she said.
    "Funny," she had been carrying the "village" of old structures around for the last twenty years. Rules, beliefs, way of seeing and doing things the proper way."

Breaking the glass ceiling had been actually easier than breaking her own: the invisible ceiling in her head. This internal set point reminded her what "her place" was.

Success, money, and income all a symbolic reflection of beliefs about personal and professional market value. And what socioeconomic class you are in. Or trying to be in.

Shopping, yes shopping too ...

· · ·

The first time Gabrielle brought home a brand new Chanel bag was like taking home a brand new baby, the fruit of your hard labour and love.

Walking into the Chanel boutique on New Bond Street was like a dream: the plush and pristine environment, the sophisticated smell, and the sales associates a populist version of Chanel mannequins.

I can't believe handbags smell. But they do. I still remember the subtle unmistakable waft of calf leather when the associate opened THE box of a brand new 11.12; the double clasp, the interlaced metal chain and leather, the diamond quilting, the softness yet sturdiness of the leather. It represents so much more than a bag. Look at me; look at what I've become.

"I'll get this," she said, handing over her credit card. She did that without asking for the price. Gabrielle walked out of the boutique with her feet barely touching the ground, almost skip-ping. The exhilaration of that purchase was like a potent drug, the high overpoweringly seductive.

But with every high, there is a low and the need for one more fix.

"God, I had a few." Fixes. Chanel, LVs, Prada, Louboutins. Each time the high was lower, and each time the effect was briefer.

And now they are all sitting in pretty boxes in the wardrobe.

It has been a time of forced simplicity; you could say Covid-19 has taught us how to pare back and reconnect with the things that really count. Who would have thought we didn't need to buy that many bags or shoes?! Go figure!

Sitting in pyjama on zoom calls, somehow you don't need that much. Just need to remember to stand up slowly when the camera is on.

NOTE TO SELF: THE CAMERA IS ON,
KNICKERS ON THE SCREEN NOT A GOOD LOOK.

Just like that, everything changed. Everything that was so important is not as important anymore.

Was it ever?

Symbols, worth, survival: feelings powering actions.

The Working-Class Millionaire worked very hard for his money. I guessed when he started to earn more than his inner worth set point, he had to work harder. Longer hours. Or somehow sacrifice more to make it feel fair.

That was one of the first things he ever told her when they first met.

"He is a m-i-l-l-i-o-n-a-i-r-e", his mouth filling up.

How much money he makes, how much everything he owes costs. That made Gabrielle cringe, so *déclassé*.

· · ·

He constantly tried to surpass his father, a working-class immigrant who made a fortune post-war. Never actually believed he could.

She could never understand at the time how an investment banker had such an aversion to money and being wealthy.

He never quite adapted to his new habitat.

The concert had just ended, and the foyer was buzzing, all talking about the amazing performance. Gabrielle herself was still euphoric from it. Beethoven's 9th symphony had this effect on her, lifting her spirit and soul to a higher place.

She admired the orchestra's incredible artistry and skill but was mainly flooded with emotions. Not usual for her; passion requires vulnerability, and we can't show weakness, can we?

"So what did you think? Did you like it?" Gabrielle asked the Working-class Millionaire.

"I'd rather have my eyes scratched with a needle."

"Pardon?" Gabrielle turned her head slightly.

"I didn't grow up with this music; it doesn't do anything for me. It is music for pansy people."

"Not many people grow up listening to Beethoven or classical music on a daily basis. Nevertheless, you can't deny how magnificent it is. Even more so as Beethoven was deaf when he composed it."

"That figures; it sounded like it."
    Gabrielle could just hear him now. Was he serious?

The crowd proceeded slowly toward the exit of the Barbican Centre, hurrying them along Silk Street.
    As they walked hand in hand, they couldn't have been more apart. Gabrielle was, for once, glad to be amongst so many people.

As much as Gabrielle wanted to leave her past behind her once and for all, he was clinging to it, carrying it with him wherever he went. Where and how he grew up defined him like an indelible mark.

Gabrielle was always striving to improve, and that attitude was inconceivable for her.

She couldn't quite understand how one would want to remain a moth instead of becoming a butterfly.

Gabrielle had risen to the top of the corporate ladder and was enjoying every minute of it. Unfortunately, Mr Working Class Millionaire had to go.

. . .

The Stud was tall and muscular with deep green eyes and voluptuous lips, which he knew how to use perfectly: the spark between them was instant from the moment they met.

The way he looked at her made her feel like the most beautiful and desired woman in the world. The fact that he was several years younger than she was made it all even more exciting, talking about men-in-power-with younger totty in tow. Except for this time, she was the one in power, and the man was the totty.

God, sex was good. I wonder why I thought about that now. "Must be the rain; it always puts me in the mood."

The thrill, coupled with the validation, was a potent aphrodisiac - the gentle stroking of the ego between the gentle stroking of the nipples.

As an introvert, Gabrielle was generally happy on her own – the pandemic made her miss-doing things with other people (shocking). One of those is definitely sex. But, unfortunately, self-love works only for a while...

Their first time was in a hotel room at a Company conference. The hide and seek, the sneaking around, added to the thrill. Their public, professional relationship giving way to a steamy and passionate relationship in private. Secret sex, secret encounters, a relationship hidden from the world.

And at the beginning, it was fun and exciting, but after a while, it became tedious; she wanted a proper relationship - who wants to spend every weekend alone?

"I should have known, all the signs were there, and I ignored them."

Something was always happening at the weekend. Gabrielle confronted him once and asked him outright if he was having an affair.

"How can you say that?" The Stud said, and he then started crying.

Seriously?

A cancer survivor in remission, he was getting anxious each time his check-up was coming closer or his mum called (I suppose that's what you get when you go out with boys). But, however big or small, something was always happening at the weekend.

Blah blah ... blah blah ... blah blah blah.

"God, I sound like a real bitch here."

His cancer was his Linus blanket. Gabrielle had thought of leaving him so many times, and each time the sob story would come out, so she stayed. She didn't want to be the heartless cow that left him when he was down in the dumps, depressed. Should have.

NOTE TO SELF: ALWAYS LISTEN TO INSTINCT.

Six months after they finally split, she came across a charity website and there it was: a picture of a couple who had a very successful fundraising event - The Stud and his girlfriend. The problem was that the fundraising event took place when they were still together.

"WE were together, not THEM."

An affair, my ass! I WAS THE OTHER WOMAN!
Fierce competition for jobs is one thing, but this went against all her principles.

Gabrielle felt sick, literally S-I-C-K.

She sat in her bath and scrubbed and scrubbed and scrubbed for hours and hours until she felt clean and remotely better.
She was so mad she even dreamt of killing him a few times in the most painful way (note to self, plot for a book) and in the slowest way possible (book series). Then downgraded it to chop his dick off.
"That could do."

"I guess a twatt with cancer is still a twatt."

She took her bowl of coffee and sat there, resting her hand for a minute. The men in her life had been a projection of her inner thoughts, beliefs and perception.
What she always thought was an outer game was really far more an inner game. This was never more apparent than when she met The QC.

. . .

Gabrielle had spent her morning perusing Islington Farmer Market on Chapel Market, looking for a variety of fresh produce, local delicacies and organic foods.

Then a bit of window-shopping at Little Paris to look at some eclectic range of vintage, curiosities, contemporary fashion and home accessories directly sourced from France. She was nervous thinking about tonight for the first time in a long time.

"This one could be good."

She amused herself with a spot of lunch at Salut on Essex Road.

Islington residents are spoiled with the local food scene, with very few areas offering so many restaurants and so many great places to eat, and Gabrielle's love for food was fully indulged.

She loved Salut's open kitchen, watching the chefs creating the magic - locally produced meat, sustainably sourced fish, and organic vegetables, all mixed with incredible passion.

The food was wonderful, the portions on the small side but completely worth it. The atmosphere intimate & friendly.

She chose the Pan-Fried Scallops, Pig's Trotter & Green Apple Declination.

Just a starter.

She didn't want to feel too full or look bloated: the dress she would wear was not very forgiving.

"Time seems to go so slowly today."

. . .

"Why is it that sometimes months go by like days and hours feel like months?"

She took a long shower to freshen up, and then she could start getting ready. It was three o'clock now, and her date was at seven.

"God, another four hours."

She took her time to get ready. Dressing up, but not too much. Sexy, but not too much. Fitting for Sunday evening drinks. Just a touch of red lipstick in an otherwise almost make-up-free face to show a bit of effort. But not too much.

"I am naturally this beautiful, right?!"

Five o'clock.
   A lot of time.
   Six o'clock.
   Spritz of perfume.
   Six thirty.

Gabrielle started to leave the house. A last glance at the mirror to check everything was as supposed to. Her sleeveless black dress, just above the knee, revealed enough of her slim but curvy figure and her long slender legs. The knee-high boots complemented the look perfectly.

She waved her hand at a black taxi passing by. "Knightsbridge, The Mandarin Oriental, please," Gabrielle said to the driver.

As they arrived, the porter opened the taxi door.

"The bar, please."

"Turn right there on the left, ma'am."

Ma'am??? God, did I look that old Gabrielle thought? Never mind.

The bar was dark and atmospheric, an intimate setting as if it had been purposely staged for romantic rendezvous. A few couples were sitting here and there, enjoying drinks and nibbles. One man was sitting at the bar alone. He turned his head as if he knew she was arriving and smiled, pleased with what he saw.

And so was she. The QC was just like his picture. Authoritative, distinguished and masculine.

He stood up and greeted her warmly (thank God he was tall), a kiss on each cheek, "You smell amazing," he said as he was *breathing* her in.

He ordered some bubbly. Nice taste. Gabrielle loved bubbly. Expensive one. She chooses to drink it often, not just on special occasions, a signal to others that her whole life is a special occasion, someone who stands on the outside of crowds.

For a first date, everything seemed to go amazingly well; the conversation was flowing, flirtation and banter with the occasional casual touch.

She was dubious when she first saw his profile on the Encounters Dating site without a picture. Mind, she didn't put up a picture either, but that was different.

"I don't really want everybody to know my private business or be recognised," he had said, "I am a very public figure."

· · ·

They exchanged numbers and pictures quickly, and he disclosed his full name and the website link for his Chamber so she could Google him. What were we doing before Google? God knows.

She googled him all right: divorced three times, made Silk in 1999, endless landmark cases won around the world. Described as a genius.
The famous QC. Perfect.

"What are you looking for?" he asked.
"Someone smart that I can talk to about anything and everything. Someone attractive, and by that, I mean that I am attracted to. Someone who has his life figured out, I don't want a rescue project. And someone who has bigger balls than I have. Definitely. I want to be the girl in a relationship."
She regretted saying that as soon as she said it.
He nodded and waved his finger in the air: "Tick, tick, tick. Three out of four isn't bad."
"Which three?" and they both smiled.
"I like you. I feel like kissing you."
Did he just blush saying that? Gabrielle looked closely. Perhaps it's just the lights in the room. But, nope, he was definitely blushing.
"Why don't you?" Gabrielle hinted. He leaned forward and kissed her gently on the cheek.
"Listen, I wasn't expecting this date to go on for too long. For a first date, I normally schedule half an hour or so. You know, just an introductory first drink."

SCHEDULE???

. . .

"But now, I don't want it to end; I'm having too much fun. I'm hungry, though. I was going to stop at Waitrose, get a couple of steaks and then watch Downton. Care to join me? I would love that."

Wait, did the QC just say he is watching Downton Abbey?

"At your house, you cooking..."
"Yes," he said.
"Can you cook? I mean, has anyone eaten your food and is still living? And talking to you?"
"Cheeky. Steak, salad and a glass of red. Or two. I promise I will be on my very best behaviour."

Gabrielle thought how crazy that was. She had just met him, a complete stranger, but she felt safe and comfortable.

"I can't believe I did that, the irresponsibility of youth," she reflected. She'd be horrified today if her niece did that.

They arrived at his house in South Kensington; actually, mansion is a far more fitting description. Everything was just as she imagined: a fabulous open-plan Boffi kitchen with quartz worktops, Gaggenau appliances and glass sliding doors leading to a show-stopping west-facing garden with a Japanese maple tree, patio heaters and built-in seating, marble bathrooms, wooden flooring, air conditioning, inbuilt smart TVs, electric blinds, underfloor heating and security system.

· · ·

"I sound like an estate agent here. How odd that I remember that."

The evening went by far too fast, and when it was time to leave, he called her a taxi.

"Islington, please", and quickly handed the fare to the driver, the perfect old-fashioned gentleman, "Make sure she gets home safe."

"Yes, sir."

"Text me when you get home." And so she did.

The QC was absolutely brilliant, and Gabrielle enjoyed the long debates they had. She was proud he was comfortable talking about his cases and asked her opinion. Made her feel really good about herself, on par.

His mind was absolutely mesmerising. His ego, however, was ginormous, and he was unequivocally self-centred. A man used to live life on his own terms, with people around him accommo-dating every single one of his whims.

That's how Gabriele liked it too. It was unbearable. Mostly because it was like looking in a mirror and not quite liking what you see.

He was leaving for Hong Kong in a few days, a very important case. Everything he did was always *very important*.

"Come tonight; I want to see you."

. . .

He was going for a couple of months, and she was going to miss him.

She could have easily got dressed and gone to spend time with him. But she was ready for the night, face off.

"He's f***ing unbelievable," she thought, "how dare he? Does he think I do not have commitments?"

She didn't go. And just like that, everything changed.

It was the beginning of the end. Everything that could have been and never was.

Looking at yourself in the mirror and liking what you see is much harder than one thinks. Looking at yourself in the mirror and loving what you see even harder. Perfection is so hard to achieve, and trying to be perfect all the time is exhausting.

Always striving, never arriving.

Like the Champagne Socialist: working class, uber gifted, scholarship for Eton, EVP in one of the Big 4 consulting firms, and still suffering from Impostor Syndrome.

Gabrielle met her Italian friend Paola for a spot of lunch at Trullo, a lovely tiny restaurant just around Highbury Corner on St. Paul's Road.

Food, wine, attention to detail – Trullo is a neighbourhood Italian, serving simple, affordable River Café-style food at a fraction of the starry Italian, a two floors contemporary trattoria with a reputation for fresh pasta, charcoal grilling, and gorgeous tarts. If it wasn't for the London buses and traffic outside, you could even think you are in some trattoria in Italy.

They both loved its big, bold flavours from great ingredients presented in a simple non-pretentious manner.

"Lunchtimes are calmer usually," Paola said, looking around perplexed.

"Sugar, I forgot: it's the pre-Gunners home game rush from the champagne-socialist-city types-Arsenal supporters."

"What are you like? Champagne socialists? PS: one of them is actually looking at you. Don't turn. He is coming over."

I guess boy meets girl meets boy is not much different at twenty, thirty or forty.

And so he came over, Mr Champagne Socialist. Cute.

The Champagne Socialist was spending Christmas with Gabrielle and her family. She really liked how family-oriented he was, and he was getting along really well with her mother, which was a definite plus.

They had lunch with his children on Christmas Eve at his favourite restaurant, Le Boudin Blanc, a French restaurant located a short walking distance from Green Park tube station and the main road, a big family affair.

. . .

The smell of bacon and eggs wafted through the air. Gabrielle breathed in the aroma.

"The neighbours are having breakfast," she thought. She took a sip of her now warmish coffee.
> Food, so many memories linked to food.
> "I miss eating out."

The Champagne Socialist was a foodie himself; only the best restaurants would do, Michelin starred mostly.

We had been at Le Boudin Blanc several times before, for lunch, dinner, after drinks, etc. . and I loved it each and every time (and the extremely generous portions).

As soon as you venture down Trebeck Street, you are transported in charming and picturesque alleyways – an oasis of calm amidst the hustle and bustle of city life, where leisurely business lunches are *de riguer* together with some people watching - literally speaking, if you sit outside on the pavement.

Watching the world go by with nice food and wine is one of the best past-times. "God, I miss eating out."

"*Pour moi, Moules marinières à la crème et Confit de joues de porc, Jésus de Morteau, poitrine de porc fumée et cassoulet de haricots coco si vous plait,*" Gabrielle said to the waiter, in French of course.

. . .

The lunch went swimmingly well; the service was excellent, with perfect timing both for serving/clearing and giving enough attention to the diners but not too much to feel intrusive.

The evening was equally as glorious: Christmas Carols by Candlelight at the Royal Albert Hall followed by midnight Mass - a Christmas tradition for Gabrielle and her mum. Again, the Champagne Socialist fitted in so well.

NOTE TO SELF: REMEMBER TO CHECK IF SOME RESTRICTIONS WILL BE LIFTED FOR THIS CHRISTMAS.

They exchanged gifts at midnight. Gabrielle opened her gift from CS: a chunky silver vintage bracelet with Murano glass. A quirky creation meant to appear bohemian and crafty, despite being so obviously expensive.

Everything he wore was designer, the type of clothes with no label, simple, but you have to mortgage a house to buy them. And he was buying in bulk.

Obviously, so him. Obviously, not Gabrielle. At all.

She remembered seeing it when they were browsing shops in Covent Garden, looking for presents for his daughter and his dizzy sister.

. . .

"You don't like it, do you?" mum whispered after he had left the room. Gabrielle raised her eyebrows with a faint smile.

Mum still wears it all the time; she loves it.

It had taken some time for Gabrielle to realise that how she ultimately saw herself had governed her life.

She wanted to change. She needed change. She needed to change.

Sometimes it takes a great emergency or crisis to delve deep and discover how much more you can do. Or should do. Gabrielle was not afraid to make big choices: she left her big corporate job in the middle of the pandemic and now taking her time to figure out what she really wanted.

She started to treat her body and herself with love and kindness, no more torture and self-flagellation with super hard schedules. Nothing to prove now.

Émile Coué talked about the power of self-suggestion, and Gabrielle had been on working on just that. Like a method actor, she had fully immersed herself in her new character, finally releasing her mental shackles.

She was disciplined and committed. To herself. Until her new identity becomes part of her. Until it becomes her.

Everything can change, just like that.

· · ·

If Covid-19 had taught her anything, it's that you can't put your life on hold and wait for the future. The road called "someday" leads to a town called "nowhere."

The happily ever after can be hers. Everything and everyone you meet is really just you.

And everything did change, one day, just like that ...

Gabrielle had ventured further out for her walk, further than the usual Islington confinement. She lost track of time and space listening to a podcast and her affirmations; she walked, and walked, and walked.

Down St John's road towards St Paul's.

She could see St Paul's from afar, standing tall, majestic, like a beacon. She remembered how much she loved attending the service there and listening to the Cathedral's Choir perform.

She was zigging and zagging from side to side to avoid the people she came across on the streets. Everyone was looking at each other suspiciously. Masks or no masks.

A few ambulances coming out of the gates at St. Bartholomew hospital.

The One New Change was deserted, "How depressing."

She enjoyed walking around London like a tourist.

"Gosh, how long has it been now?" She had lived in London for twenty years now and never felt at home anywhere as much as here. Her heart was full of gratitude.

You can lose yourself in the streets of London; every day, discover new nooks and crannies. Follow the River Thames down to the Tate or Borough Market.

"St Paul's will do today."

Gabrielle had been alone through the lockdown; her parents were technically in her bubble but still living in the village up North.

"A bubble indeed."

She had a few trusted friends in her inner circle, but they all had their own families to think of. Gabrielle is the only single in the group. She had been single for over a year now. In the end, she decided she was better off alone. At least until she had worked on herself and was truly deeply sure about what she wanted and needed. Better off alone than with the wrong man.

She made un café allongé with a slash of double cream to take with her.

"Why did she do that?" She never ate or drank on the go. I guess not being able to stop at will had something to do with it. Or it was just fate.

She poured the hot, fragrant mixture in her portable coffee cup and off she went on her long walk.

"I am a Goddess, I am a Queen," her affirmations playing in her ears. Gabrielle was taking her time, savouring every moment, every view.

Is there any other time but now? Amazing how much you can see when you are really looking.

. . .

She was absorbed in herself, finally standing in her own power as a fully embodied feminine woman, knowing that to be adored and be treated like a Goddess, you need to first realise you ARE one. No need to act like a man anymore.

It had been a long journey, but she was finally arriving at her destination. Finally, she was ready to say "Yes" to life in its entirety, comfortable in her body and emotions, embracing ALL of herself.

She was lost in her thoughts, sipping her coffee as she turned around the corner ...

BANG! Ouch ...

The collision was surprisingly strong, considering they were both just walking. Gabrielle had lost her balance, but he was quick and promptly grabbed her by the waist to keep her from falling.

The coffee wasn't that lucky and splattered everywhere.

E-V-E-R-Y-W-H-E-R-E on her white dress.

"Life is not happening to me. Life is happening for me", she kept repeating in her mind looking down at the brown spots on her dress, "Bummer, coffee stains, and I'm nowhere near home."

They were so close now. He smelled really good.

"*I am a Goddess* ..." still playing in her ears.

. . .

"I am so so sorry," he said. Gabrielle looked up, his piercing blue eyes shining, his dazzling smile peeking through the mask half down his chin. He looked firmly, steadily, straight into her soul.

"At least he is cute," Gabrielle thought. "Thank you, Universe."

"Are you OK?" he seemed genuinely mortified by what had happened.

"I'm OK, thank you. Not a big deal, really. It is only coffee," playing it cool.

He was staring at her. She didn't know if to back up to keep some parvence of social distancing or hold the stare. Fuck it. Hold it.

She felt like getting closer instead. She didn't.

"Let me get your dress dry-cleaned for you," he offered.

"Dry cleaners are closed."

"OK, at least let me wash it for you."

"Really, it's only coffee; it's not a problem."

Gabrielle wondered if he lived in London or got stuck here when the lockdown started. He had a distinctive North American accent, New York, she thought.

Judging, judging, stop it, Gabri. Every Tom, Dick and Harry lives in London; everybody has an accent here, including you.

"No, really, let me do this for you. I live just around the corner: I can wash your dress and have it ready back to you in a couple of hours. Perhaps even make your coffee while you wait. One that you can drink this time," he insisted.

. . .

Wait, did he just ask me back to his place and offer to wash my dress?

She squinted with her deep dark eyes staring into his and said:

"Is this a cheap ploy to see me naked?"

"No, no, no, YES "... mortified "No, no. I mean, it would be great, but no."

She smiled profusely. "I feel like I'm in a scene from the Vicar of Dibley: where is the camera?"

"What?" obviously not getting the reference.

"Sorry, British cultural reference. I'm kidding. I'm OK, seriously, no need to go through that much trouble. It is only coffee."

"I want to. I was hoping to spend more time with you ... perhaps a date tonight?"

The upfront American; quickly glanced at his hands to see if there was any appearance of a wedding ring. Both hands, to be sure.

"Restaurants are closed too."

"I can cook." Dejavu.

"Social distancing?"

"I think we broke that rule already. We can eat alfresco if that makes you feel better," he added.

"I don't really know you."

"I'm trying to remedy that," and sensing her reluctance, "Can I have at least your number?"

. . .

Gabrielle was intrigued and totally attracted to him, and so she did. He had just finished tapping her number into his mobile when her phone started ringing in her pocket.

"Are you going to get that? he asked.

"Pardon?"

"Your phone, are you going to answer it?"

"No, it's rude; I am talking to you. I can see who called me later."

"It's me."

"You can't be missing me already; I'm still here," she said, grinning and gesticulating.

"I just want to make sure I have the right number. And you now have mine, too," he was grinning too. "Are you sure I cannot convince you to have dinner with me tonight?"

"Not tonight."

"Another night then. Tomorrow?"

Gabrielle smiled. God, this felt so good.

"I better go now" she smiled again, waved and started walking away.

She hadn't felt like this in a long time. Actually, ever. Her body was on fire, her spirit soaring.

"What just happened there?" she was walking on clouds.

It would have been the perfect exit had she not turned around to see if he was still there. But she couldn't help herself.

He was still there, standing still, looking. Smiling.

As she turned around the corner, her phone vibrated, a text:

"Now, I am missing you."

"That's understandable," she replied.

And just like that, that day, everything changed. A few months have passed by now, and Gabrielle ...

BANG!

"Babe, I'm home."
The American, Mr Wonderful, peeked into the room to say hi, his sparkling blue eyes gazing at her. Soaking from the morning run. Water dripping on the floor.

"You are soaking wet."

"I'm going to have a shower," he said with a cheeky grin "want to join me?"

"Obviously," Gabrielle said.

I guess morning pages are done for today.

With love
- Gabrielle

"OUR SELF-IMAGE, STRONGLY HELD,
ESSENTIALLY DETERMINES WHAT WE BECOME"
- DR MAXWELL MALTZ

PART I

THE NINE LIVES OF GABRIELLE: FOR THREE, SHE PLAYS

To New York, one of my three loves

A NEW YORK ADVENTURE

THE NINE LIVES OF GABRIELLE: FOR THREE , SHE PLAYS

G abrielle was getting ready to go out.
A surprise from Mr Wonderful.
Out for dinner and then to the Opera. Going out again felt incredible after almost two years of off-and-on lockdowns. They were celebrating the day that they met. He was always full of surprises: spontaneous, romantic and thoughtful.

She hadn't had the time to think carefully about what to wear and was getting ready at the last minute. Finally, she decided on wearing the same dress she wore when they met: the white dress culpable for so many mischiefs, the dress that started it all.

Albeit it was so lovely to go out again now that all the restrictions had been lifted, it was also so strange seeing a mix-match of people with and without masks everywhere you went. The anxiety and slight fear when hearing someone coughing. You can just see the suspicion on people's faces. "Has he/she got IT?" The new dreaded C-word.

However, slowly and surely, life is getting back to normality. Time is passing by, and life needs to go on. She missed travelling and going out. Socialising and the theatre, she loved the theatre, and Mr Wonderful knew her well.

BANG! Ouch...

The collision was surprisingly strong, considering they were both just walking. Gabrielle had lost her balance, but he was quick and promptly grabbed her by the waist to keep her from falling. Unfortunately, her coffee wasn't that lucky and splattered everywhere.

· · ·

E-V-E-R-Y-W-H-E-R-E on her white dress.

Memories. The smell of coffee and cologne. He smelled really good. Affirmations were still playing in her ears when they banged into each other.

"I am a Goddess; I am a Queen"
    - very empowering, perhaps a tad scary for a man to hear when they first meet you.

"I am so so sorry," he said.

"Gosh, thank you, Jesus, he is so handsome,"
    Gabrielle thought as she looked up at the piercing blue eyes, the dazzling smile peaking through the mask now half down his chin.

Gabrielle felts like he was looking straight into her soul. He was genuinely mortified by what had happened.

"I'm OK, thank you. Not a big deal, really. It is only coffee," she said, playing it cool.

He didn't stop looking straight into her eyes, not even for a second. She didn't know if to back up to keep some parvence of social distancing (and decor) or hold the stare. Fuck it. Hold it.

. . .

She felt like getting closer instead. She didn't. He offered to get her dress dry-cleaned for her. Gabrielle wondered if he lived in London or got stuck here when the lockdown started. He had that distinctive North American, New York accent.

"Please, let me do this for you. I live just around the corner: if the dry cleaners are closed, I can wash your dress and have it ready in a couple of hours. Perhaps even make you a coffee while you wait. One that you can drink this time,"
    he insisted.

"Wait, did he just ask me back to his place and offer to wash my dress?" pondering,
    "This is the type of exchange you see in Hallmark movies. Or the real crime police dramas."

She squinted with her deep dark eyes staring into his and said:

"Is this a cheap ploy to see me naked?"

"No, no, no, YES." .
    ... mortified
    "No, no. I mean would be great, but no."

She smiled profusely and felt like teasing him.
    "I feel like I'm in a scene from the Vicar of Dibley: where is the camera?"

. . .

"What?"
looking puzzled and obviously not getting the reference.

"Sorry, British cultural reference. I'm kidding. I'm OK, seriously, no need to go through that much trouble. It is only coffee."

And then he asked her on a date. Gabrielle remembered how she quickly glanced at his hands to see if there was any appearance of a wedding ring. Both hands, to be sure. And no, there was no ring or signs that he was wearing one regularly either.
He offered to cook too.

"What about social distancing?"
Gabrielle said.

"I think we broke that rule already. We can eat outside if that makes you feel any better or safer,"
he said.

"I don't know you."

"I'm trying to remedy that,"
and sensing her reluctance
"Can I have at least your number?"

Gabrielle was intrigued and attracted to him, so she gave him her number. He had just finished tapping her number into his mobile when her phone started ringing in her pocket.

. . .

"Are you going to get that?" He asked.

"Pardon?"

"Your phone, are you going to answer it?"

"No, it's rude; I am talking to you. I can see who called me later."

"It's me."

"You can't be missing me already; I'm still here,"
    Gabrielle said (he is keen, a good sign).

"I just want to make sure I have the right number. And you now have mine too,"
    he was grinning too.
    "Are you sure I cannot convince you to have dinner with me tonight?"

"Not tonight."

"Another night then. Tomorrow?"

. . .

He was sure of himself without being arrogant and persistent. He knew exactly what he wanted and was going for it.

Gabrielle felt really good about the encounter and excited as she hadn't been for a long time. She remembered waving and walking away. Actually, she had never felt like this before. Her body was on fire, her spirit soaring, and she was walking on clouds.

It would have been the perfect exit had she not turned around to see if he was still there. But she couldn't help herself. She had to.

He was still there, standing still, looking. Smiling.

As she turned around the corner, her phone vibrated, a text:

"Now, I am missing you."
   "That's understandable," she replied.

Just like that, that day, everything changed. He was everything she always wanted but wasn't quite ready for before. And it was still going.

"Honey, are you almost ready?"
   Mr Wonderful asked, peeking through the bedroom door, "the Uber will be here in the next few minutes."

"Where are we going exactly now?"

as it was too early for the Opera.

"Dinner."

"I know, you said. Where, though?"
Gabrielle, the in-control planner, needed to know.

"I made a reservation for Balthazar in Covent Garden."
Nice, and within walking distance to the Royal Opera House. She had mentioned to him that she had been in New York; he must have remembered.

Balthazar was busy. Very.

They were greeted as the walked in and taken straight to their table. The relatively small room, with faux-nicotine-stained walls, a station clock, and the poised amber hue, is almost made for Instagram.
There was a lively buzz in the air.

Just as well, Mr Wonderful had made a reservation because there was a queue outside waiting to be seated. Many who tried a walk-in turned away, disappointed with the wait.

Gabrielle ordered the mussels for the starter and steak tartare for the main course. Mr Wonderful had ordered champagne seemingly on tap to wash everything down.

· · ·

He was soo good at remembering all the little details and celebrating every occasion, no matter how small or big. Anything she ever said, he listened and acted upon. She was speechless because he remembered so much about everything she had told him.

He was spontaneous, romantic, thoughtful, and passionate, with piercing blue eyes. No wonder Gabrielle called him Mr Wonderful.

They were seated in the right-hand corner of the restaurant, just in front of the bar, with a good view of the room and the window, great for people-watching, should you want to.

They could barely hear each other lost amongst the live jazz, the chitchat and the noise of plates and cutlery, but, at the same time, it was very intimate and cosy. Even in the middle of a crowd, Mr Wonderful only had eyes for her.

Chitchat, chitchut.

The same sounds different vibe.

Clink clink … clink …

Gabrielle adored grand set-piece spectacular restaurants with ambience. Balthazar is undoubtedly that and perhaps, one of the best brasseries in London for its atmosphere, happy, friendly staff and service, living up to the reputation of his New York City original.

. . .

The first time she had visited Balthazar in New York was on the weekend for brunch, steak and eggs, New York pancakes and Balthazar Bloody Mary.

The VP took her there. They had only just met a few days earlier.

skahdeedath bideedoodop... gahdugat ...

"NYC Balthazar is much bigger than this one", was going through her head.

It was amidst the full Sex and The City hype at that time. A place everyone wanted to be seen at.

And the VP made sure they had the most visible table in the room.

He was waving at people, smiling.

"You see that man on the corner?"

Gabrielle turned her head slightly to see what he was talking about.

"He is the CEO of such and such .... Major client."

"That one over there is the anchor of NBC News,"
name dropping
"and that blonde woman over there is in a famous soap opera."

. . .

People watching. Or, even more important, been watched. They were seated bang in the middle of the room, which was definitely good for that. Not a great table to have a conversation and get to know someone.

Then again, Gabrielle didn't think that was why they were there.

That was the first date with the VP after Gabrielle arrived in New York.

The trip was a last-minute decision after a long-term relationship breakup.

Another failed relationship.

Gabrielle had reached boiling point and felt claustrophobic. She needed to escape, have an adventure, re-group and re-think what she would do. She felt like she had thrown five years down the drain. She had given everything she could and had nothing more to offer right now.

"Let's get married and have babies,"

he said out of the blue, after five years and all the previous talk about a commitment that went nowhere.

Unbelievable. Too little, too late.

. . .

Mentally she had moved on. She wasn't sure anymore if she saw a future with him. Growing old with him. Or as the father of her children.

Her friends always told her,

"Why don't you get pregnant?
You know, a-c-c-i-d-e-n-t-a-l-l-y. Things happen all the time, and you'll at least have a child."

Gabrielle knew that some (many? few?) women do that, and sometimes it works well. Sometimes not so much.
But she, she could never bring herself to do it. To even try.

There are enough unwanted children in the world, and bringing another potentially unwanted one in didn't feel like an option to her. Although, to be fair, she was always planning for her career, move after move, and it never quite seemed to be the right time to get pregnant.
Moving town, travelling, and finding a new bigger job always sounded more like desirable and viable options.

Perhaps she didn't want a child.
The idea of a child, yes. The idea of being a mother, yes.
Doing it not so much. She had thought that having children was so ingrained that she had to want it; being a mother as the pinnacle of being a woman. She always wanted to be free.
Always wanted to travel, free to do what she wanted, when she wanted.

. . .

Marriage too.

The idea of an all-encompassing, consuming, can't-live-without-someone love affair was thrilling. A strong man to look after her. Finding a man she could bear 24/7 without feeling trapped, not so much. And now, all she wanted was to take off.

Just go somewhere.

New York - the Big Apple dream - had always been lurking in the background. This was the perfect opportunity to take the plunge. So she wrote to her boss requesting time off and got her tickets. Three months in New York, a mini-sabbatical. Longer than a holiday but short enough not to need a working visa.

On her taxi ride to the airport, she felt like Indiana Jones

(OK, mini Indiana Jones); it was her first-ever trip alone, non-work-related.

Not visiting anybody. Nothing planned. Just her and New York.

Exhilarating and scary AF.

The flight felt much longer than she imagined, maybe because she had to squeeze between two enormous individuals overflowing into her seat. Perhaps because they never stopped moving, talking, or eating. ALL the way throughout the flight.

"Jesus, what's wrong with actually keeping quiet for a few hours. Or just sleep,"

she asked herself, already knowing the answer. To Gabrielle, it felt like people were afraid of silence and desperately needed to fill in.

. . .

"God knows what they are afraid will happen if they are alone with their thoughts. So most of the time, people fill the void with absolute total nonsense. And unfortunately, on a plane, there isn't much of an escape route. You have to listen. Well, kind of."

Chitchat, chitchat, blah blah blah…

And constant eating.

"Really? Who brings snacks on a long-haul flight? I'm sure starvation will not sneak up on you if you don't constantly munch on something. Out loud. The airline already provides food, starvation prevented."

Note to self: MUST book business class for the return flight.

As the plane landed at JFK, people proceeded calmly out of the aircraft, following the different signs directing toward Customs and Border Protection. Brits are good at queuing, and it comes naturally. Whilst the passengers were arriving near the actual desks, Gabrielle was jilted out of her thoughts:

"Ma'am, step behind the yellow line."

"Is she talking to me?"
Gabrielle thought. "Did she just call me Ma'am?"

. . .

She didn't know if she was more upset about being called Ma'am ("do I look that old?"), especially as the officer didn't look that much younger herself or being shouted at by an overbearing sturdy officer WITH A GUN.

Apparently, she was doing something wrong. Gabrielle didn't know what it was, but it seemed to have annoyed her. A lot.

The Border Protection officer got closer to Gabrielle, far too close for comfort because she was sure they weren't about to *faire la bise* and proceeded to shout, again, explaining,

("I must have looked really tick", she wondered),

"Ma'am, step behind the yellow line. You have been admitted into the United States only once you have gone through my colleague at the desk. Step behind the yellow line."

"What? Really? I'm pretty sure the plane landed at JFK, and JFK happens to be in the US of A. So what is she going to do? Throw me back into the sea?"

As all these thoughts were going through her mind, Gabrielle sheepishly said,

"Sure, no problem, officer."

she didn't feel that courageous to argue with an armed, angry person in authority.

The reputation of trigger-happy American police (whatever) is infamous and, unfortunately, or fortunately, was imprinted in her mind. She also had images of being locked up without contact with the external world and sent back. Or kept somewhere.

God knows where.

"I have watched too many police movies,"
Gabrielle thought.

What a contrast from the officer behind the desk.

He was a young male in his late twenties or early thirties, seemingly shy. And he was unlucky enough to have three ladies who had just landed from Manchester at his desk. They were having a great time, which seemed to have started on their plane, or before, with copious alcohol. So one might say they were "tipsy."

And determined to have a good time.

New York was their stop the night before embarking on a Caribbean cruise. They were officially on holiday, probably FROM Manchester. They must have been in their late fifties, early sixties, or at least what looked like sixty or thereabout in Gabrielle's mind. They were making all sorts of advances to the poor guy who, by now, had become red-faced up to his roots.

And was getting redder by the minute.

They were totally shameless, and who can blame them? He was cute, wearing a uniform (which always helps) and reinforced by each other and vodka martinis.

. . .

He couldn't wait to get them off his desk soon enough.

Bless.

Then came her turn. Gabrielle was sure she had never been asked that many questions going through any other customs in any other country. At least she couldn't remember. Neither did she think they sounded legitimate questions (to grant entry into the country).

Perhaps he was reasserting his authority and regaining control after the cruise ladies, or maybe that's what he usually asked. Who knows.

Gabrielle preferred to think there was some mild flirtation going on. But, hey, he was cute, and it was a friendly welcome to New York. She felt smug and almost tempted to turn back and poke her tongue out at the

"Step behind the yellow line" officer but thought perhaps better not.

She stepped out of the airport and looked for the taxi lane.

"324 West 44th Street, please. The TownePlace Suite Manhattan, please.

let the adventure begin.

. . .

As they drove toward the city, the taxi driver made small talk. Gabrielle was distracted: she was soaking in the atmosphere, excited about what the next three months would bring.

She had chosen an extended-stay boutique-style hotel right in the heartbeat of NYC's Times Square and within walking distance to Broadway, Restaurant Row, Macy's Herald Square, Empire State Building and many other famous attractions.

She wanted to have the most authentic experience possible in a neighbourhood-style accommodation with a kitchenette.

Of course, New York is full of places to eat everywhere, and she could easily go out for dinner if she wanted to. However, she both liked the convenience and pretending she was living there, if only for a little bit.

Perhaps cook a few meals from time to time.

Come to think of it, Gabrielle had never been out for dinner or in a pub by herself.

E-V-E-R.

Even when meeting people, she always checked to ensure they arrived first.

"Baby steps, Gabri, baby steps,"
she said to herself.

. . .

She flew in early in the morning to enjoy almost a full first day and then crashed at "normal" sleeping time to beat the jet lag. She arrived at the hotel around 2 pm and, after a quick shower and change of clothes, she was ready to start exploring.

Gabrielle had bought an Insight New York City Pocket Map. She had studied on the plane and planned a few days out.

"I know it's an adventure, but some structure won't go amiss."
     She had been trying to decipher the New York street system …

"Odd-numbered streets go west, and even-numbered streets go east. Right, OK…. And odd-numbered buildings are on the north side of the street, and even-numbered addresses are on the south. So streets run east to west, and avenues run north to south. I think I got it."

She ventured to Time Square, then the New York Public Library on Fifth Avenue and then a little spontaneous wander for her first outing.

Everything was so new and yet so familiar. She recognised buildings and streets at almost every other turn.

Hello there, she thought as a handsome guy was walking by, going in the opposite direction.
     "Talk to self; you just arrived, Gabri. Give it time."

.   .   .

As they crossed each other paths, the stranger smiled at her, a dazzling smile. He wasn't her usual type. She usually liked the tall, dark, handsome ones (or blonde) but definitely tall. She was 5.5ish and liked wearing heels.

He was more of an average height, a.k.a. shorter, with a soap opera-ish all-American look.

"Nice shoes", he said.
Interesting pick-up line.

"Pardon?"
Gabrielle replied.

"You look like you're walking with purpose. Are you going somewhere specific?"

She didn't want to give too much away; he was a perfect stranger, after all. For all she knew, he could be Jack The Ripper or Ted Bunty. And before she could answer,

"I'm on my way to the office for a meeting. Here is my card with my cell and office extension. Can I meet you for a drink later on?"

Mmmmh …

. . .

"Or perhaps a coffee tomorrow morning?"
he said as she looked pensive.

OK, that sounded more reasonable. Gabrielle was still hesitating.

"You can come into the building where I work and ask for me, and then we can go for a coffee?"
Better. Definitely better.

"Let's say 10 am? How does that sound?"

"Sounds like a plan", she replied.

"And what is your name, lovely lady?"

"Gabrielle."

"Nice to meet you, Gabrielle. I'll see you tomorrow. Bye."

VP OF CORPORATE FINANCE - said the business card. VP uh? Not a bad start for an adventure.

The second morning she had the American breakfast at the hotel; she wasn't quite used to having breakfast in the morning, but she thought it was better to have one considering she had planned a long day out walking—eggs, bacon, sausage and pancakes.

. . .

She had contemplated all night if to go and meet the VP.

"What have I got to lose? It's just coffee and a chat in a public space. What's the worse that can happen?"

His office was in a massive building (aren't they all) in MidTown Manhattan by the Rockefeller Center. The receptionist buzzed his office extension to let him know Gabrielle was there.

"You look lovely today,"
he said. He smelled of fresh cologne and had a crisp blue striped shirt, making his eyes stand out.

"Let's go. It is only a few minutes away, right down the steps from 1 Rockefeller Plaza. There is a nice coffee bar with espressos and very nice coffee in general. You'll like it."

He was very talkative and wanted to know more about Gabrielle. Not too much, but more. The VP was making plans for the weekend. Brunch at Balthazar.
We can do this. We can do that. Plans for the two of them.
A bit presumptuous.

Mind, it was her first weekend in New York, and she quite liked the idea of having some company. Moreover, the fact that she was there for a limited time made it more appealing.
Probably to both of them.

. . .

Time flew quickly. He had to return to the office, and they agreed to meet outside Balthazar. Gabrielle had plans to walk some more and had studied her map. She was so proud when someone who looked like a tourist asked her for directions.

"Success."
Everything was going so well until she reached the West Village, and then it went Pete Tong,

"What happened here?"

The familiar grid-like street system was nowhere to see. As she walked around, she stumbled on the Magnolia Bakery. She got a couple of cupcakes to see what the fuss was about.

Gabrielle tried to look for familiar landmarks and streets to get back to the hotel.

"I'd be damned if I get out the map,"
she said to herself. She could have easily reached for a taxi, but she wanted to walk. Needed to walk.

She arrived back at the hotel exhausted and went straight to bed. Day two was over by 8 pm—rock'n roll, baby.

. . .

She woke up in the morning and took the time to savour her coffee and enjoy the New York view, still not believing she was actually here.

"Time to get ready for brunch."
That day was the beginning of her affair with the VP.

He became her chaperon with benefits. He knew how to live and have fun. The high New York life.

Their relationship grew into a whirlwind, inhibited affair.
She felt like she was in a movie that, one day, would end inevitably—all more exciting for it.

Theatres. Cinemas. Museums.

Gabrielle got to know the most famous spots in New York. And got to have sex there too.
The VP bought her a lot of gifts. Perfume. Flowers. Jewellery. Money was his "love" language. Lots of lingerie. He loved Victoria's Secrets. She had to clear a drawer just for it.

He was the perfect chaperon and was not shy in introducing her to his acquaintances.

"This is Gabrielle, my *friend* visiting from London, England,"
he would introduce her.

· · ·

The VP took her to his place in the Hamptons too. He had a house in Cooper's Beach.

Gabrielle had heard of the Hamptons: the towns and villages on the eastern end of Long Island in New York state, a popular getaway for people from New York City.

When the VP told her the Hamptons were in New York, she was perplexed. It took them about two-and-a-half hours by car to get to Westhampton, where the Hamptons start.

Two-and-half-hours!

And to reach the end of the island's South Fork is another 50 miles east.

It's like saying Manchester is in London.

"Perspective, Gabrielle, everything is a matter of perspective," she thought.

Gabrielle could see why so many wealthy and famous spend their summers here: ocean breezes, white sand beaches, excellent seafood, lively parties, the rural atmosphere of Long Island's South Fork and the more laid-back Southampton Town.

For the weekend, the VP had planned a visit to the Shinnecock Golf Club, one of the historic golfing institutions in the United States, apparently.

. . .

Even though it has been renovated and expanded, its character remains substantially the same as a century ago. An accompanying member must sign in all guests;

obviously, the VP was a member. He also bought her the appropriate golf attire and briefed her on the Club's strict rules.

"Hello, are you there? Honey?"
Mr Wonderful said.

"You seem miles away. Are you OK?"

Gabrielle was yanked back into present London.

"Yes, yes, I was just enjoying the food and lost in my thoughts,"

"I hope he hasn't been talking about something important, and I missed it," she thought.

They finished their pre-theatre dinner and strolled toward the Royal Opera House around the corner. Hand in hand. Like the day they met, the electricity between them was palpable. But was it too good to be true? Sometimes she doubted she deserved him / it.

They were going to see Madame Butterfly, the fascinating and heartbreaking story of words and promises carelessly spoken with inevitable consequences.

Un bel dì, vedremo
Levarsi un fil di fumo
Sull'estremo confin del mare
E poi la nave appare
Poi la nave bianca .....

The VP had taken Gabrielle to the Metropolitan to see Madame Butterfly. Because he loved Opera, better still, be seen at the Opera, the best seats of course.

"I love this aria,"
he said.

It is incredible how the same experience can differ at different times. The music transported her in and out of her body, back and forward in time.

....Entra nel porto
Romba il suo saluto
Vedi? È venuto!
Io non gli scendo incontro, io no
Mi metto là sul ciglio del colle e aspetto
E aspetto gran tempo
E non mi pesa
La lunga attesa

Mr Wonderful looked at Gabrielle and kissed her gently on her forehead,

"Io sono qui, e non mi pesa la lunga attesa. Io ti aspetto."

SEARCHING FOR GOREN

THE NINE LIVES OF GABRIELLE: FOR THREE, SHE PLAYS

"Io sono qui, e non mi pesa la lunga attesa. Io ti aspetto," said Mr Wonderful whilst looking at Gabrielle and kissing her gently on her forehead.

The singer was belting one of Madame Butterfly's most famous arias, Un bel dì, vedremo:

> *E non mi pesa*
> *La lunga attesa*
> *E uscito dalla folla cittadina*
> *Un uomo, un picciol punto*
> *S'avvia per la collina*
> *Chi sarà, chi sarà?*
> *E come sarà giunto*
> *Che dirà, che dirà?*

She smiled, not knowing what to say. Sometimes Mr Wonderful could read her mind, and right now, she was sure he knew she had been miles away.

Madame Butterfly always had the power to take her back to her mini-sabbatical in New York and the performance she saw at the Metropolitan Opera in the Lincoln Center.

The auditorium combines old-world elegance with sleek contemporary, with around 3,800 seats and 245 standing-room positions. The acoustic is superb.

Grandiose.

· · ·

For Gabrielle, though, the Met is just too big. Instead, she prefers the Royal Opera House in London, with 2,256 odd seats offering a far more intimate experience.

Like New York - London. The VP and Mr Wonderful.

Madame Butterfly with the VP was a show, an occasion to get dressed, socialise and be seen.

With Mr Wonderful was a moment to cherish if she could only stop being dragged back.

Is the past ever gone? Memories intrude the present moment, fantasies dropping into the continuous present of our lives.

Everything is always present. Vivid imagining sometimes feels more real than reality itself.

How easy to be confused.

The New York trip kept popping into her mind, intruding.

A last-minute decision after a long-term relationship breakup. Gabrielle needed to escape, have an adventure, re-group and re-think what she would do.

On her taxi ride from the airport, she felt like a mini Indiana Jones on her first-ever trip alone, non-work-related. Not visiting anybody. Nothing planned. Just her and New York. Exhilarating and scary AF.

. . .

She had decided to go for three months, longer than the usual holiday but short enough not to need a working visa.

It seemed like a good idea at the time.

By the second month, the novelty was wearing thin without a job or friends to meet and the VP at work during the day.

Gabrielle had walked Manhattan from top to bottom and east to west. She had almost memorised every street.

Well, it certainly felt like it.

She had met the VP on her first day there, and they had been going out since. He had taken her to all his haunts and introduced her to all the right people (HIS right people)

—the perfect chaperon with benefits.

She was bored.

Holidays are relatively short periods that one plans. This New York trip had been unexpected, totally unplanned and without any schedule. Gabrielle was always used to having something occupying her mind, side by side, with a very active social life.

She was so bored that she started watching television far more than she was used to back home, flicking from channel to channel (far too many).

. . .

She often settled for the Law and Order franchise, something familiar to watch, always been a fan of murder mysteries and crime dramas. Gabrielle was particularly fond of Law and Order Criminal Intent and one of its characters: Detective Robert Goren, played brilliantly by character actor Vincent D'Onofrio.

Detective Goren was tall, dark and handsome, moody and incredibly perceptive in a Sherlockesque deducing manner.
He also is totally screwed up in his relationships.

In other words: perfect and her usual type.

To pass her time, she started googling to find out where they were filming, if any filming was going on, and which actor was filming.
She considered going too.

Reddit seemed the place to find out together with every possible D'Onofrio/Goren sighting, the two more and more intertwined in Gabrielle's mind. An intelligent and attractive hero right here in New York. Where she was right now.

She was almost living a double life.
By night living the sparkling New York City life with the VP.
By day searching the internet for the latest place where Goren had been seen:
- Bond St,
- Stuyvesant Town,

• Bleecker Street …

One day, she read that he was a regular in Tompkins Square Park, Christodora House, so she walked down from MidTown and stayed there for hours.

H-O-U-R-S.

Waiting.

Nothing happened, of course, besides that she had turned into a semi-stalker.

Then, on her way back to the TownePlace, she saw him. Right at the intersection of Third Avenue and 14th Street.
    Goren was driving a big dark Range Rover.

Ok, no clue what car it was, a big one. Her heart was beating fast. She actually saw him. Live.

And, just like that, he was gone. Just like that, Gabrielle had turned into an obsessed teenage stalker.
    Splendid.

God knows what she thought she would do had she properly met him. Fall madly in love and move permanently to New York. Or him moving to London? She hadn't thought that far.

. . .

She was searching for something and not finding it. She hated to admit that she was always going for emotionally or physically unavailable men.

What if she was always choosing people who don't allow intimacy? Was it because, deep down, she didn't want it?

Or was she afraid she'd lose herself entirely if she let herself be loved?
Was SHE the one afraid?

How could she stop hooking up with emotionally unavailable people? People who can't actually love her.

And now, here she was, with Mr Wonderful.

Right here, right now, the most physically and emotionally available man she had ever met.
Totally devoted to her.

She could see a common denominator when she looked back at her quasi-relationships that didn't work out.

Herself.

. . .

The Working-Class Millionaire who worked very hard for his money. And the more he earned, the harder he had to work to balance out his low inner worth set point.

"He is a m-i-l-l-i-o-n-a-i-r-e", his mouth filling up.
    One of the very first things he ever told her.

He constantly tried to surpass his father, a working-class immigrant who made a fortune post-war, but he never believed he could.

She never understood how an investment banker had such an aversion to money and being wealthy.

Truth be told, he had never quite adapted to his new habitat.

But, on the other hand, Gabrielle was always striving to improve, and that attitude was inconceivable to her - she had left her village behind,
    both mentally and physically.

She couldn't quite understand how one would want to remain a moth instead of becoming a butterfly.

The Stud was tall and muscular with deep green eyes, voluptuous lips, and a voracious sexual appetite.

. . .

The fact that he was several years younger than she made it even more exciting, talking about men-in-power-with younger totty in tow.

Except for this time, she was the one in power, for a change, and the man was the totty.

The thrill, coupled with the validation, was a potent aphrodisiac. And at the beginning, it was fun and exciting, but after a while, it became tedious; Gabrielle wanted a proper relationship, not every weekend alone.

And even though all the signs were there, she ignored them.

He was a cancer survivor in remission who used his cancer as his Linus blanket.

Gabrielle had thought of leaving him so many times, and the sob story would come out each time.

She had fallen for someone with so many red flags that he could have been an air traffic controller. But she continued to see him, giving him the benefit of the doubt.

She didn't want to be the heartless cow that went to him when he was down in the dumps, depressed.

. . .

Six months after they finally split, she came across a charity website and there it was: a picture of a couple who had a very successful fundraising event -

The Stud and his girlfriend.

The problem was that the fundraising event occurred when they were still together. Gabrielle had been THE OTHER WOMAN.

Then came the QC. The famous QC.

Smart, attractive, with his life totally figured out. And someone with bigger balls than hers.

But, in insight, they were too big.

The QC was brilliant, and Gabrielle enjoyed their long debates, proud he was comfortable talking about his cases and asking her opinion.

His mind was absolutely mesmerising. His ego was equally ginormous. A man used to live on his terms with people around him accommodating every one of his whims.

That's how Gabriele liked it too. It was unbearable, mainly because it was like looking in a mirror and not quite liking what you see.

The Champagne Socialist followed. Another mirror but, this

time, not liking that much of what you see. Perfection is so hard to achieve, and trying to be perfect all the time is exhausting.

Perfectionitis is a terrible disease.

Always striving, never arriving.

Gabrielle had kept looking, convinced she'd find someone who wanted to be with her because she was *special*.

Like the Champagne Socialist: working-class, uber-gifted, scholarship for Eton, EVP in one of the Big 4 consulting firms, and still suffering from Impostor Syndrome.

They were the same man. They were HER. Gabrielle was afraid of getting hurt. It was not them.

It was her.

Truly opening up to someone and having them reciprocate is an intimate bond. What if the relationship fails?

They were perfect and the safe option. Since they were guarding their emotions closely, there was a decreased risk of emotional engagement. AKA getting hurt.

Gabrielle couldn't deny that the thrill of the dating chase was fun.

. . .

Wanting what you cannot have it's a never-ending, dead-end chase with intermittent positive reinforcement. Up and down. Reward and withdrawal.

Committed to not committing.

And in New York, she was living a fantasy in her head that didn't require putting in an effort to make an *actual* relationship work.

So the VP was the holiday fling and Goren, Goren, was the ultimate emotionally unavailable person, someone she "couldn't have" because he didn't actually exist.

A television character brilliantly interpreted. That's all.

And now this fantastic man was in her life, and she couldn't find any faults. He was present and engaging more deeply, authentically and emotionally. Mr Wonderful had never made any promises that he hadn't kept. He was there, fully, completely, emotionally and physically available.

Ed egli alquanto in pena
Chiamerà, chiamerà
"Piccina, mogliettina
Olezzo di verbena"
I nomi che mi dava al suo venire
Tutto questo avverrà, te lo prometto
Tienti la tua paura

Io con sicura fede l'aspetto

As the heartbreaking song was coming to an end, a tear started rushing down her cheek.

"It's ok", he said, "it's ok.
Io sono qui, e ti aspetto."

TASTING FREEDOM

THE NINE LIVES OF GABRIELLE: FOR
THREE, SHE PLAYS

I t was the weekend, and Gabrielle reflected on the night out with Mr Wonderful. He had arranged dinner and Opera tickets to see Madam Butterfly, one of her favourite operas, to celebrate their meeting day.

Only a few months had passed since they moved at lightning speed. From meeting in the street to dinner/date to being in the same bubble in the last lockdown. And after that, he never left.

He seemed to remember every moment they had: their first meeting, first kiss, the first time they made love, their first weekend together. And celebrate it.

This amazing man in her life engaged in a more profound, authentic and emotional way than she had ever experienced. Fully, completely, emotionally and physically available.

Getting to know Gabrielle was like peeling an onion's multiple layers. She understood this about herself. She has had friends for over ten years who have never been to her house. Always kept something back. *Truly* opening up to anyone requires a level of intimacy she wasn't used to. And never liked. It required vulnerability.

The smell of coffee permeated the room at the NoMad London hotel. He had thought of that too to continue the celebration into the weekend. Right in Covent Garden adjacent to the Royal Opera House, in the Bow Street Magistrates' Court Building. Splendid.

. . .

"Good morning, darling," he said, just back from the fitness centre. "I'm going in the shower. Want to join me?"

Dejavu.

"Obviously", she replied.

"How are you this morning?" Mr Wonderful enquired. His voice had an underlying worrying tone. Gabrielle had to do something to reassure him. Her mind wandered off and on all evening.

London - New York -London- New York. A round-the-world trip in one single evening. Better still, a round-the-world trip in her memories and back.

She felt so guilty.

New York had been an essential step in her life. The action that ultimately got her here today.

Becoming the woman she was today, albeit still a work in progress.

Three months where she did not have the single-vision focus of her career but allowed herself to grow. In whichever direction. A last-minute decision to take a New York trip after a long-term relationship breakup turned out to be one of her best decisions to date. Besides giving her phone number to Mr Wonderful.

"Can I have your number?"
   he said, and then he called her straight away.

"You can't be missing me already; I'm still here,"
   Gabrielle told him, teasing.

"I just want to make sure I have the right number. And you now have mine too,"
   grinning from side to side.
   "Are you sure I cannot convince you to have dinner with me tonight?"

That was, for sure, her best decision. But New York was a close second.

Three months in a different city in another country led to further thinking. But, you take yourself wherever you go. Gabrielle did just that initially and started a brief affair post-arrival that lasted almost two months.

But eventually, she came to her senses. She decided to REALLY explore the city. Not just the usual suspects like Central Park, the Statue of Liberty or the Empire State Building but also, for example, the small breakfast cafe around the corner that served the biggest breakfast she had ever seen.

.   .   .

She walked in alone. Sat down with no distractions or barriers and ordered. What seemed like the smallest item on the menu.

"A cheese and ham omelette, please."

After a short time, the most humongous plate of food arrived at her table.

"Excuse me," she said. "I'm sorry, I think this is the wrong order. I asked for a cheese and ham omelette?"

"That's right," the server said. "That's it, honey."

The plate was overflowing. God knows how many eggs were used; probably a whole battery of hens was at work here. And there were chips, bread slices, and so on.

Gabrielle struggled to finish the omelette and left all the "garnish" behind.

"What's wrong, honey?"
    the server looked worried.
    "Was there something wrong with the food? You left the majority behind ... Do you want to take it away?"

"Good Lord, no", Gabrielle was thinking. "Far more carbs than I have ever seen in my life."

. . .

"I wasn't that hungry; it was delicious, thank you,"
she said aloud and made sure she left a generous tip behind.

She also learned to wander the various neighbourhoods, slow
and purposeful walks to get to know the area, even better,
people. She was not afraid to ask questions and be seen as the
tourist she was. Or someone just learning. Shocking.

She stopped seeing the VP around her second month in New
York and started to go out. Alone. Dinners. Theatres.

She even booked herself into a writers' conference, something
she had always wanted to do.

The VP didn't take it very well. Not that he ever wanted to
pursue a long-distance relationship, but he was at least counting
on keeping the relationship going until she departed.

At the writers' conference, she met many people, most
Americans, a mix of professional, semi-professional, amateurs
and wanna-be writers. All extraordinarily nice and friendly. All
were extremely surprised but supportive of her first trip alone.

"You are here alone?"

. . .

"Yes, I am. I am not visiting anybody. And I had nothing planned, nowhere specific to go when I arrived" proud moment.

Gabrielle felt great about herself now. Even better, knowing that everyone recognised she had been courageous. However, they didn't realise that the scariest part of her trip had been walking into a restaurant for dinner alone. For the first time ever.

Much harder than travelling across the world. The inner battles are always the hardest and the most satisfying when you win.

And the second most challenging thing was the realisation that the men she had dated, their red flags, were her red flags. They just carried them around for her. And she had decided it was time to put them down, once and for all.

All the men she dated were the same man.
    They were HER.

They were exactly right for her each time because they were safe and presented no real risk of ultimately getting hurt.

Gabrielle realised she had been committed to not committing.
    "That's a commitment for you," she thought, smiling.

Slowly but surely, in the same New York where she lived the fantasy of pursuing Detective Goren, she slowly broke her shackles.

. . .

"I'm good darling, Terrific. Never better,"
she said, smiling. "I think I owe you an apology."

"No, you don't. I just want to know you are ok, that we are ok."

"Absolutely," she said." So, let's have that shower and then a chat?"

"It's not one of those 'We need to talk' moments, right?"
Mr Wonderful asked.

"No, no, no ...."

"Vicar of Dibley?" he asked, smiling.

"No, no, YES ... no," she replied, smiling.

After a long, steamy shower, they went for a walk and just like that, Gabrielle started talking.

For the first time, really talking: she told him about New York, the why, the when and the how. She told him everything.

Ok, not E-V-E-R-Y-T-H-I-N-G.

. . .

She omitted the chasing Vincent D'Onofrio/Goren around NYC like a crazy person.

"This onion needs to keep some layers,"
    she thought. At least for now.

And as their day ended, her shackles were falling even more, and Gabrielle was finally tasting freedom.

Freedom is an elusive concept. Some men hold themselves prisoner even when they have the power to do as they please and go where they choose, while others are free in their hearts, even as shackles restrain them.

-- Brian Herbert

PART II

THE NINE LIVES OF GABRIELLE: FOR THREE, SHE STRAYS

To Paris, one of my three loves

PARIS TOUJOURS PARIS

THE NINE LIVES OF GABRIELLE: FOR THREE, SHE STRAYS

G abrielle woke up, the sun filtering through the gap in the heavy curtains.

They were back home after a long weekend celebrating. Celebrating in more ways than one.

The day before, after dinner and the night at the Opera, Gabrielle had finally started to open up to Mr Wonderful. They were out to celebrate the day they met—another of the many surprises from Mr Wonderful.

He was still asleep, and she couldn't stop looking at him, fearing he would disappear like a *mirage*. How lucky she was.

And how afraid she was going to screw this up too.

Mr Wonderful lips were slightly arched as if whatever he was dreaming of made him smile. His thick dark eyebrows framed his masculine face perfectly. A strand of hair covering his forehead and just a little stubble from a few days without shaving covering his face. He smelled soo good: a mixture of his cologne and after-sex pheromones. His arms were still around her, as he couldn't quite sleep without being close to her, skin to skin.

He was very handsome and, from his facial expressions, looked like he was having a perfect dream.

Gabrielle was lying there, motionless, trying not to breathe, not to wake him up. Precious moments. She loved them and savoured them. No questions asked. Just contemplating how lucky she was. Especially after talking, aka talking about herself. They spent the previous day talking, or at least it had felt like a day to Gabrielle.

She had to.

. . .

She had spent the whole time whilst they were at dinner and the Opera wandering in and out of her consciousness, back and forward from her past. And he had noticed. Of course.

He was always so attentive. "Too much sometimes", thought Gabrielle. She'd prefer if he couldn't read her so well. But, unfortunately, what she had always craved was here, and it was not as easy as she had hoped. Intimacy is a bummer.

She always liked to present the best of herself. The best of herself she wanted the world to see. Being laid bare was excruciating.

"Good morning, gorgeous,"

Mr Wonderful said, flashing one of his dazzling smiles. Perfect pearly whites. His blue eyes pierced through her soul.

"Good morning,"

She purred and sunk her face into his chest, trying not to look into his eyes. He knew she had done enough talking, at least for now, far more than she was used to, so he held her firmly, stroking her back whilst kissing her forehead.

"I love you,"

Mr Wonderful whispered, "Always."

Gabrielle looked up for a minute and replied,

"I love you too, more than I can say."

"I know."

They stayed in bed some more, lingering.

The crumpled bed sheets around them.

After some time had passed, she got up and started getting ready for her morning walk. One of the few habits she developed during lockdown that she kept after starting her relationship with Mr Wonderful. But, of course, you can't exactly run an overnight tape with 'I am a Goddess' affirmations when you are sleeping next to someone you are remotely interested in—or can't sleep either with one of those gizmos with Bluetooth, still not very sexy.

But she kept the morning walks and writing her morning pages. She started carrying a notebook on her walks and occasionally stopped to write her thoughts. Whatever came to mind: anything and everything.

Mr Wonderful was a gym-type of person, so she used that time to do her own thing.

"Darling, I need to write some papers for work. Do you mind if I use your office?" he asked.

Ever so polite, he understood how precious Gabrielle was with her space, house, and things. Between falling deeply in love and lockdown, they practically moved in together almost immediately. He was wary of not "overstepping" and being overfamiliar. He was determined not to take anything for granted.

"Not going to the gym?" Gabrielle asked.

"Maybe after I finish work, I have a deadline."

"Sure, I am going for a walk."

"I'll be here," Mr Wonderful replied.

Gabrielle always enjoyed walking, especially down the canal. Being near the water, the sounds and the smell made her feel at peace and relaxed. She often stopped and sat to write her morning pages while watching the canal and the locals' daily lives. The water was standing still...

"Be still and know that I...," peacefully meditating in the moment.

. . .

The door closed behind Gabrielle, and Mr Wonderful jumped out of bed and into a quick shower before getting ready to do some work.

With a fresh cup of coffee in his hand, he then proceeded towards the small crook in the corner of the house that Gabrielle had designated as an office. There it was, where Gabrielle did all her work, painting, writing and filming for her YouTube channel. A foldable antique lacquered screen was concealing the area.

Clear boundaries, "So Gabrielle," he thought as he folded the screen away and sat at the desk.

He powered up his laptop, checked his emails and then the stock exchange, followed by a quick call to his broker to sell and buy some stock and shares. The desk was just by the window, looking over Canonbury Square and Canonbury Gardens.

He found himself wondering.
Wondering how hard he had fallen for her and how fast.

How she walked into his life out of the blue. He had never met anybody before this enchanting, enthralling, and so elusive.

His previous long-term relationships had always played the second field to his business and personal interests: cars, racing, and flying. And now, all he wanted was Gabrielle.

Her big brown eyes had captivated him from the first moment; her perfume seduced him, and her voice sealed the deal.

But, most of all, it was her sweetness and vulnerability hiding behind the strong, badass facade.

Yes, she was beautiful, almost hypnotising, even more, because she was playing it down and self-deprecating. She didn't fully realise the effect she had on men or him. When she walked into a room …

"Boy, I have fallen hard," he thought.

"I need paper. Where does she keep printing paper?" he asked himself.

He looked into a few drawers of Gabrielle's exquisite French cabinet, which she used as a desk.

"Nope," pens, highlighters, pencils, brushes but no paper. "Ah, here it is," he said as he opened the last drawer.

As he took the A4 paper out of the drawer, he noticed something that looked like a folded note. Maybe something Gabrielle had written recently …

"I shouldn't look," he thought, reminding himself how private she was.

But the letter bated, called him and tempted him to read it. For hours he resisted and kept on working. But he couldn't concentrate. He was distracted. The letter kept popping into his mind.

Then, finally, he gave in; he made another cup of coffee, sat down and unfolded the inviting note.

"Ma chérie Gabrielle, n'aie pas peur de combien je te désire."

· · ·

Mr Wonderful French was rusty but understood a few core words like "*désire*". He searched for Google Translate on his laptop and typed the words with apprehension.

"Dear Gabrielle, don't be afraid of how much I desire you," read the first line.

His heart was sinking, and his mind was going awry.

"When was it written? Where is the date? There is no date in this letter," he thought.

He cursed himself for not paying more attention to the French classes in school and not practising more French with Gabrielle. The process of translating phrase by phrase was excruciatingly painful. So slow. Mr Wonderful's mind was playing with his heart when he noticed that Gabrielle was standing right there, looking at him, looking at her, the letter unfolded in his hands.

Gabrielle couldn't help but notice his expression. The colour had drained from his face.

Gone was the loving look he had earlier on. Instead, Mr Wonderful looked stone-faced, almost grey; his eyes were red and swollen.

"Has he been crying?" she thought. "What is he reading?"

It was then she noticed the open drawer where she kept THE letter. *Le PDG* wrote it to her when he feared that their love affair would end soon.

Paris, Toujours, Paris taunting her.

. . .

After the New York sabbatical, Gabrielle felt reinvigorated with a new perspective on life. In the last month in the Big Apple, she had thoroughly worked on herself and done some introspection.

Gabrielle had always shied away from getting too deep into anything: relationships, herself, and life. So she never understood how she always stopped on the verge of greatness, on the brink of enormous success.

Something always happened, somehow, and she couldn't see the pattern. But now, everything looked so painfully clear. Too painful. Gabrielle had so many shields and layers that she wasn't just protecting herself from the world. She was keeping herself from the world.

Back in London, in familiar places, everything, however, looked so different. She remembered escaping from her "village" and arriving in London only to confine herself to another "village", barely getting out of it. A self-imposed upgraded cage, which now was feeling claustrophobic.

Gabrielle was back at work and ready for new challenges. Work had always been her safe place, where her achievements spoke for themselves, with her identity firmly rooted in them. Work had been her life.

Her phone rang.
"Did you have a good time?"
Her MD asked.
"Yes, thanks, fabulous!"
She replied.

"Are you going all American on me now?"

He smirked. "Can I see when you have a minute?"

"Sure, I have a gap in my schedule after lunch. Sheryl has already planned my life for the next decade,"

Gabrielle said.

"Yes, your P.A. is very efficient. After lunch, it is fine."

Gabrielle caught up with emails and read the summary prepared for her. Sheryl had been sifting through her emails while Gabrielle was away and diverting them to the appropriate team member.

"What would I do without my Sheryl?" she said.

After looking at the latest report on market share and preparing for the meetings in the afternoon, Gabrielle took some time for lunch. She could have easily met the M.D. over that hour, but her P.A. had blocked time so she could take care of herself, eat properly and not just gulp something down whilst talking about work. She was behaving more like her mother every day.

Knock, knock...

"Come in", the M.D. said. "Coffee?"

"Yes, please," said Gabrielle.

"When you were in New York, lots of changes happened, some moves, some people left," he started, clearing his throat.

"Yes, I know; Sheryl has filled me in. I have seen the announcement for the departure. Interesting," she replied.

"Usual announcement in this type of case," implying this particular one hadn't been a 'voluntary' leaver.

"Well, with all these changes," he proceeded, "there are now empty positions, you know ... opportunities," looking at Gabrielle intensely.

"I imagine so," she said. The penny hadn't dropped yet.

"What's going on with you?" he asked. "What happened in New York? You would have knocked at my door. Hell, putting it down to talk to me about opportunities before."

She squinted her eyes.

"Well, never mind. There is a permanent position opening in Paris, working with the main Board of Directors for the Group and *Le PDG,* but the role is based in France. So what do you think?"

Gabrielle was happy to be back at work and in her element but, for once in her life, she hadn't quite thought or planned her next move. At least not yet.

"I love Paris. It sounds interesting. I just bought my house in London,"

She said tentatively, thinking a permanent move to France was not exactly what she had anticipated.

"You know the company helps with relocation, finding a place and so on..."

"Yes, I know."

"So, what do you think?" he repeated.

Gabrielle knew that if you truly wanted to advance your career in the company, you had to handle the acquisition and integration of a new company into the Group, the French way, and have worked in France. At least for a bit.

They were the unspoken rules. Paired with the other unspoken rule that all company directors throughout the Group have to speak French.

Although English was the commercial language of the Group

if you met *Le PDG* or presented to him and the Board, you did so in French.

"If you are interested, they are interviewing next week in Paris. First, second and third interview on the same day."

"Validating?" she kind of asked, but not really.

"Yes, that's right. Validating."

Gabrielle knew French working culture well and the politics that come with that. It was the differentiating factor that got her job role: that and the fact she was bilingual. Gabrielle worked as Marketing and P.R. Director for the Group branch in the U.K., the not-so-unspoken rebel.

France wanted the U.K. branch to be managed the French way, but the U.K. was having none of it. So they needed an in-betweener to bridge the cultural gap.

"Why don't you leave then? "

Gabrielle said during a U.K. board meeting to one of her colleagues, the Sales Director.

Everybody turned to look at her, astonished that she had said that aloud.

The Sales Director was a middle-aged Scottish man who had worked for the company for twenty years, ten before the company was acquired by the French Group.

In ten years, despite lessons, he still couldn't string two French sentences together. Gabrielle had lost her (French) patience with him.

He was not feeling appreciated, blah blah blah ... the French this, blah blah... the French that, blah blah blah...

• • •

"If you don't like it, why don't you leave?"

She repeated.

"In this day and age, companies should recognise their employees," he kept moaning.

"You are not an employee. You are a Board Director. And that's not the culture! This is a French company. More direct, *combative* and with far less sugar coating. You are expected to do well. It is a bit like school and parents going to meet their children's teachers to find out how they are doing. The teacher will not sing the child's praises and tell the gushing mother how wonderful the child is.

Non, the teacher will point out what the child is not doing well. Because they are expected to do well within the confinements of their age group. Same as you are expected to do well in a job you get paid handsomely to do. You are not going to get praised for it too. Get over it."

They all looked at her like she had just made a significant revelation.

"Sorry all, but that's the way it is."

Gabrielle was so French when in London and so British when in France.

She would need to get used to politics and all the sycophants that worked with *Le PDG* pretty fast.

The Group Board of Directors was a mix of old schoolmates of *Le PDG* or people who had risen through the ranks from when his father was at the company's reign.

He had grown the company from a small artisan one in the north of France to one of the most prominent in the country. Now, *Le PDG* had expanded it globally, acquiring an average of one or two companies per year every year.

• • •

Gabrielle was presenting for the first time to *Le PDG* in her new capacity and wanted to make an impression.

She researched the subject thoroughly and prepared stats and figures to support her proposed strategy. Her presentation was in English, but all the handouts were in French, and she presented in French. She dressed up for the occasion, too: more feminine than she would have in London but pared down, letting her mind do the talking.

The office was in *Tour Montparnasse* with a spectacular view of the *Tour Eiffel*. The room was set up in a traditional presentation style with *Le PDG* placed right in the middle of the table, his right-hand and left-hand men on each side, and then in order of importance and inner circle closeness. He was known in the company for asking many questions; the unspoken rule to anyone presenting to him was 'know your figures or suffer the consequences'.

"A bit dramatic," she thought, but she nevertheless memorised all the figures and handouts, just in case.

Le PDG was in his early forties and had been leading the company for at least ten years. He was the sole shareholder of a private, now multi-billion euros company.

He was tall and slender, wearing tortoise glasses resting on his long aquiline nose. His hair was mousy, with a hint of grey running through his temples.

He was notoriously private, so much so that there weren't any pictures of him in circulation, much to the dismay of the French press.

. . .

His anonymity allowed him to travel between *Londrienne* and Paris on the TGV on his own, unnoticed.

Le PDG looked at Gabrielle intensely as she entered the room. Gabrielle had sent copies of her presentation and collateral in advance and expected a grilling.

And she got one.

He interrogated her for hours, the only one asking the questions. All the others nodded, making the obligatory "*Oui, oui*" noises from time to time.

Gabrielle stood there, defiant, answering every question without hesitating. She had memorised every page and every figure and tried to pre-empty every question he might have. It was a duel — a hypnotic duet they were playing. His eyes never once left hers.

Penetrating hers.

And at the end "*Bon*". And the meeting was over.

As everyone started to get up and leave the room, he said:

"We are going for lunch now. Would you like to join us?"

Gabrielle wondered if this happened all the time, but this wasn't the time for questioning. "*Oui, merci*," she said.

They all left and went down the elevator for what seemed like an eternity.

The company office was on the 55th floor, just below the observation deck on the 56th and the rooftop garden on the 59th. *Le PDG* was standing right next to her, towering over her. He was intent on conversing with one of the others, but she could feel the warmth of his body.

. . .

The descent went slowly, with a stop on almost every floor. And with more people coming in, the lift was feeling more and more snuggling. *Le PDG* closer and closer.

As they walked out of the building, he started walking beside her and making small talk nonchalantly. Next, they went to one of the restaurants in the area for lunch. He sat next to her and then talked with everyone around the table but Gabrielle.

She did the same.

As they were all chatting, their arms touched, at first, occasionally and unintentionally.

Then, as the lunch went on, more and more. Gabrielle looked around to see if anyone at the table was paying attention. Still, they all seemed oblivious and immersed in the food experience.

When back in the office, Gabrielle composed herself in the ladies' room.

"What are you doing? He is THE boss, and he is married,"

She said, looking into the mirror.

"Nothing, I'm doing nothing. It was only lunch. It meant nothing."

But it did. It meant something, indeed. Things capitulated from there.

The next time they met was at a tasting for a new product line. A room full of people, but they could only see each other. They were inevitably drawn to one another, each trying to overcome their fallacies and the incongruences the situation posed to both.

. . .

Gabrielle still remembered what it felt like finding out she was the other woman with the Stud. She felt physically sick.

And *Le PDG* was a good catholic boy who had been married to his childhood sweetheart for the last twenty years. He was living in Paris, Mondays to Fridays, and travelling back to *Londrienne* to spend the weekend with his wife and their three children.

Paris was not for her, the wife; she had lived in her small town all her life and had never wanted to leave. Paris was too much for her.

She enjoyed the quiet life, meeting with her friends for lunch whilst the children were at school. He was her security and validation.

Everyone in town, in one way or another, was connected to her husband's company, and she revelled in that.

He always wanted to travel and conquer the world, and his work allowed him just that. And he did take the world by storm; nobody believed he could carry the company when his father died, let alone make it a global multi-billion euro one. So he married young because it was expected to do; their families intertwined. And she was a good wife. Better still, she was loyal and invisible.

Gabrielle, on the other hand, was everything he wanted. She was equally driven, pushing herself all the time.

He wanted her but wasn't one hundred per cent sure she would reciprocate. He thought all the signs were there, but she was a puzzle.

Gabrielle was equally attracted, like the moth to the fire but wasn't quite sure he wanted her enough to do anything about it. And he was married.

So they played their dance, sussing each other out, a life argentine tango.

And then, one day, everything changed.

"Hello Madame, *Le PDG* wants to go through the new strategy and the budget; he has an opening tomorrow at 4.00 pm", his Executive Assistant said over the phone.

"I'll have to move a meeting," Gabrielle said.

"Please do," she replied.

Gabrielle was nervous and re-looked at the presentation and her figures over, wondering what was wrong. But, everybody seemed to have liked it and the decision to progress it had been made. She went over the information over and over for the rest of the day and evening and then the next day too. She had just moved to Paris and was still finding her feet in her new role.

The meeting time came when the E.A. called to say he was going to be late; his previous meeting had overrun. Gabrielle took her time to compose herself and do a quick touch-up with some blush and a veil of lipstick, just as if she had just bitten her lips.

4.30 went by.

It was 4.45 when the E.A. called her in.

. . .

"Please sit down," as he showed her the chair on the other side of his desk. "Sorry I am late."

"It's ok," she said and couldn't think of anything else. She certainly couldn't say she was pissed off for having waited almost an hour.

They started going over the figures for the budget, and the phasing of those figures and time seemed to get by quickly when there was a knock at the door.

"Monsieur, I'm going home. Do you need anything?" his E.A. said.

"No, it's all right, thank you. Have a nice evening."

Gabrielle hadn't realised they had been talking for over two hours, and it was now almost seven p.m., and they were the only ones left in the office.

He stood up by the window, looking at the lit Tour Eiffel.

Gabrielle stood silently, not quite knowing what to do or say.

"You can see most of Paris from here. Beautiful, isn't it?"

He said, turning to look at her.

"Yes, it is,"

She replied, thinking how banal her response was, 'Yes, it is. Couldn't I have said something more interesting?'

He turned his back again and continued to look outside. Gabrielle wasn't sure if that was an invitation to join him. She decided it was. He wasn't looking like he wanted to return and continue talking business.

She started walking towards him slowly, unsure if it was the right thing on many levels. As she was moving forward, he turned and looked at her intensely, savouring her every move.

Today was the day; he couldn't hold his feelings any longer. He had to know if she felt the same.

Now.

"You are beautiful,"

He said, thinking how stupid and how vulnerable he was making himself right now. She could complain.

Worse, she could reject him. But he couldn't wait another minute.

He had to know.

"I have been unable to stop thinking about you; I just wanted to see you alone. Sorry for keeping you at work late,"

He whispered.

Gabrielle didn't know how to react. The feminist in her should have felt at least some indignation, but she didn't. The moralist in her should have been repelled, but she wasn't. Instead, she just wanted to...

And then he kissed her. Slowly and gently at first.

Her forehead, her cheeks and then her mouth. A moment suspended in time. Or so it seemed.

Hours spent kissing. They finally walked out of the office around nine o'clock. He walked her home, up to her door, and kissed her goodnight.

Gabrielle couldn't sleep that night. He had bypassed her barriers and gone straight to her core.

She tossed and turned and then watched the sunrise.

She was excited to go to work and took particular care in getting ready and found herself skipping down the pavement.

. . .

Gabrielle couldn't wait to see *Le PDG* again. When she arrived at the office, the door was shut, and the light was off.

"Strange," she thought.

Hours went by, and nothing.

No sign of *Le PDG*.

She heard in passing that he was travelling out of the country for an acquisition and won't be back until the following week. Gabrielle felt her face becoming red and had to go and collect herself.

"Stupid, stupid. Did you think he would tell you?"

She said, looking in the mirror.

Nevertheless, tears started to fill up her eyes. She took some time before returning to her desk and then shut the door for the rest of the day.

The week passed by slowly and uneventfully. Gabrielle was still decorating her new Paris apartment. She had decided not to sell her London home and was commuting each weekend. Going back to London was just what she needed; she couldn't face her empty Paris apartment alone.

The following week came by, and her diary was filled with meetings with various board members, other directors and *Le PDG*. She couldn't help but feel anger and resentment rising, the genie was out of the bottle now, and she was struggling to put her back.

They saw each other several times with other people, and she caught him staring at her when the others weren't looking.

However, he had made no effort to contact her outside work or see her alone. Gabrielle thought she was delusional, that she had imagined the whole thing, until …

Until they met again. This time alone.

"How are you?" he asked.

"Fine,"

She said sternly, "How can I help?"

As if nothing had happened. But it had. He drew closer and closer until their bodies touched.

"I missed you," he said,

"I didn't want to miss you. I was trying not to. But I did," he whispered in her ear.

"Did you miss me?"

"Nope"

"Not even a little bit?"

He started kissing her. "Gabrielle, baby, say something."

She wanted to push him away but couldn't resist him. She kissed him back. They soon were all over each other, on his desk, by the window. He had locked the door, but people knew better than to disturb him when he was in meetings.

From then on, they grabbed every moment they could.

Anywhere and everywhere during the day. And in the evenings, cooking and making love in her apartment.

They ached for each other.

Their passion was a spectacular affirmation of two minds

struggling past their incongruences and inability to consistently meet their core needs in a way aligned with their values.

But she had violated her moral compass, and now it was back to haunt her.

Paris Toujours Paris.

"PARIS IS ALWAYS A GOOD IDEA"
- AUDREY HEPBURN

ME MYSELF AND US

THE NINE LIVES OF GABRIELLE: FOR THREE, SHE STRAYS

G abrielle was standing in front of Mr Wonderful, looking at him, looking at her. He was sitting at her desk by the window with a letter unfolded in his hands.

Gone was the loving look he had when she left for her walk.

The colour had drained from his cheeks. Instead, he looked stone-faced, almost grey; his eyes were red and swollen.

She couldn't understand what had happened in such a short time when she suddenly noticed the open drawer where she kept THE letter from *Le PDG*.

Before meeting *Le PDG*, Gabrielle was a provincial middle-class girl who, against the odds, had made it in the oppressively male-dominated world.

He opened her up to sexual and emotional freedom she had never before experienced.

But, this time, she was the other woman, breaking her values to meet her needs.

After her New York trip, Paris promised more freedom.

Instead, it raised more bonds to break ...

"Dear Gabrielle,

Don't be afraid of how much I desire you. I will shield you with love the next time I see you, with kisses and caresses.

I want to dive with you in all the pleasures of the flesh so that you faint.

I want you to be astounded by me and admit that you have never dreamed of such a thing possible …

And then, when you are old, I want you to remember and tremble with pleasure when you think of me.

You make me hotter than hell... everything you do gets me hotter than hell.

You have raised new hope and fun in me, and I love you; your pussy hair I felt with my fingers, the inside of your pussy, hot and wet I felt with my fingers…

All this madness I asked of you, I know there is confusion in your silence — but there are no actual words to describe my great love.…

Last night I dreamed about you; I do not know what occurred exactly. What I do know is that we kept fusing into one another. I was you. You were me.

Then, we caught fire. I remember I was smothering the fire with my shirt. But you were different, a shadow, as drawn with chalk, and you were lifeless, fading away from me.

Please don't leave me, my darling Gabrielle. I am nothing without you."

Her cheeks went bright red, and she did not know what to say. Sheepishly, she hoped that Mr Wonderful hadn't read that far or couldn't quite grasp what the letter said. After all, his French was pretty basic …

But the look on his face told otherwise: somehow, he managed it and undoubtedly got the gist. He was sitting there, motionless and speechless. He didn't greet or hug her as he usually would.

. . .

She knew she was in trouble. Paris, Toujours, Paris still taunting her.

Le PDG wrote that letter when he feared their love affair would end soon.

It happened just after the annual Global strategy conference in *Londrienne*.

All board directors of the different companies worldwide attend the meeting as is customary. *Le PDG* had kept the company headquarters there, just where his grandfather founded it.

The Group had now reached such a humongous proportion that they were struggling to find rooms for everyone in the only three hotels in the small town.

Many were staying in the adjacent cities, and buses had to be arranged to transport people back and forward to the three days conference. Same for the taxis: there were only two privately owned ones in town, and her PA booked one for her way in advance to ensure she could get around.

"*Bonjour Madame,*" the taxi driver greeted her.

"*Nous sommes occupés, très occupés. Tout le monde et sa sœur sont venus au Vatican pour voir le Pape,*" he said smiling, making the comparison between the company and *Le PDG* and Vatican City and the Pope.

· · ·

This town reminded her of her childhood: her *Mamie* was French and had a house in a small village in Provence.

So Gabrielle and her parents used to spend every summer there. Although the two towns were in opposite directions, one in the North and the other in the south of France, the similarities were striking, as with most small French villages.

The love of a long mid-afternoon break and a slower pace of life is perhaps one of the reasons why living in France sounds idyllic to everybody outside France who wants to leave the city frenzy behind.

The pint-size suburb, however, made Gabrielle feel even smaller. Always did.

"Come to think of it," she thought, "the same could be said for the English place I grew up in."
    Different country, same cage.

When she moved to London, it was like shredding too tight-fitting skin.

She was glad the her role was based in Paris rather than in *Londrienne*. There were only 10,000 inhabitants, one cinema and one theatre: she would go crazy living there. Moreover, everybody knew everybody; most people in town worked for the company or were connected with it.

· · ·

When she was little, Paris was her dream city, and now she enjoyed the London-Paris Monday-to-Friday exchange.

There were some definite pluses of living in Paris: for example, even on basic salaries, you can afford to eat at *chich cafes*, try new dishes and chat for hours, a champagne lifestyle on a lemonade budget, so to speak.

She was renting a one-bedroom flat in the centre of Paris, just a few minutes from *Gare du Nord* railway station.

It overlooked some hot new restaurants in town, with lots of mismatched furniture, ping-pong tables, fantastic art and an impressive courtyard. She could watch some of the Paris hipsters milling around while cooking.

The flat was beautiful, with floor-to-ceiling windows and white walls, yet rent was cheaper than in London, helping to absorb the cost of her commute.

Every Monday morning, she would get up at 6 am in London to catch the 7 am train to Paris.

She discovered that by booking her Eurostar tickets three months in advance, she could get them for € 69 in return, not much more than double a weekly travel card in London.

. . .

She would get into the *Gare du Nord* just after 10.30 am, and after a few minutes on the *Metro*, she would be in the office.

From Monday to Thursday night, she would stay at the Paris apartment and keep her work wardrobe there to save on packing. By Friday afternoon, she was ready to return to London life.

Unlike on the Tube, nobody pushes past you on the *Metro*, which always seems to work. Being stressed and rushed is not the Parisian thing to do. Instead, you take time to admire the surroundings and taste the *café crème*.

Overall, Gabrielle was amazed at how straightforward this arrangement had been. Her mother was upset she was further away, while her father, far more laid back, was happy with whatever she was doing.

Her London friends found it more difficult because she had minimal time to spend with them.

Living in two cities wasn't tough if it weren't for *Le PDG*.

She had travelled from Paris with the *TGV* for the annual Global conference; many others were doing the same.

The *TGV*, even first-class, was surprisingly cheap compared to railway ticket prices in the UK. It felt like the company had taken over the train.

. . .

Gabrielle had been working closely for months with the various people organising the event as part of her new branding strategy. Everything was planned for the millisecond.

She was anxious about seeing *Le PDG* with everybody there.

She had been practising her professional face in front of the mirror because she didn't trust herself. Her feelings for him. And his wife would be there. AND his children were attending the informal dinner.

Gabrielle was trying not to think about it.
    And then it happened, just like that.

She was going over the last-minute details with the events team in the main conference room when she felt the need to turn around.

There they were: *Le PDG* and his wife.

He was showing her around, explaining the order of the day and evening, and making her feel comfortable. But, of course, she had to have her "game on", the dutiful supportive wife of the dazzling *Président* of the company.

. . .

Nathalie was tall, slender, and blonde, with long straight hair, dressed too old for her age. They had been childhood sweethearts, and she was only in her early forties.

Le PDG noticed Gabrielle was there and moved toward her to introduce them. He didn't want to, but he had to. He had just introduced *Nathalie* to everyone else in the room and couldn't avoid Gabrielle.

"How do you do?" *Nathalie* said in charming, accented English.

The two women shook hands. Her grip was firm, resolute as to say,

'I know who you are, and it won't make any difference. He will never leave me'.

Maybe she was, or perhaps it was Gabrielle's paranoia and jealousy. She had no right to feel jealous. She was the mistress.

"What a difference from before ..." she thought.

She found out she was the bit on the side six months after she had split up with The Stud, after coming across a charity website that showed the picture of a couple who had a very successful fundraising event-

The Stud and his girlfriend.

The problem was that the fundraising event occurred when Gabrielle and The Stud were allegedly still together.

. . .

She had been the other woman, unknowingly and unwillingly so.

Gabrielle was S-I-C-K sitting in her bath, scrubbing and scrubbing for hours until she felt clean and remotely better.

She was so mad that she even dreamed of killing him a few times in the most painful way, then downgraded it to chopping his dick off.

But, THIS time, she was the other woman, knowingly and willingly.

And she experienced jealousy like never before. This time, she dreamed of killing the wife instead. Not him. Never him. He had made her feel alive like never before.

Before leaving the room, they talked a bit longer about the order of events. After that, the rest of the day was a blur. Gabrielle ran on autopilot.

She didn't see *Le PDG* again until the evening, at dinner. She took her time and care to prepare for the evening; she wanted to dazzle him.

Make him see she was the one.

. . .

She picked a little black dress, caressing her body in all the right places, revealing her slender but curvy frame.

"You are the curviest skinny girl I have ever seen," he told her once. "I love your ass."

He was a bum man, definitely a bum man.

The dress was showing off Gabrielle's assets, like the mounting of a diamond enhancing its brilliance without being too much.

"Perfect," she thought, looking at herself in the mirror.

Just a smidge of red lipstick as if she had bitten on her lips, and she was ready to go.

Her table was next to the main one where *Le PDG* was sitting with his wife, brother and sister and the other members of the main Board.

Gabrielle noticed he seemed distracted. He conversed politely at the table but kept turning and looking at her. He could not stop.

He wanted her right here, right now. After that, he didn't care about anything else.

. . .

And when Gabrielle left her table to go to the ladies' room, he followed her there.

"You looked beautiful," he said.
"I want you," as he pulled her into one of the empty rooms down the corridor and locked the door behind them.

"I want you. This is torture," *Le PDG* whispered.

"We can't. It's too dangerous," she said.

"I don't care." And, at that moment, he didn't.

He had had several liaisons before, but nothing like this. They were just unattached sex.

His wife tolerated his indiscretions as long as he didn't embarrass himself publicly. She knew he'd never leave her.

But this time, even *Nathalie* could sense something was different.

He had stopped his regular evening calls during the week and was distracted when they were together at the weekend. He seemed to come alive only when seeing the children and when it was time to return to Paris.

．　．　．

And he had started going back earlier and earlier.

He used to take the first TGV on Monday mornings. Then, it became Sunday evenings. And now he couldn't wait to leave just after Sunday lunch.

Nathalie knew something was wrong but didn't know what she could do.

Sex had never been her thing, and she was glad he had bothered her less and less as the years went by. Travelling wasn't on top of her list either. She didn't have his intellectual capacity or depth, and they didn't share many interests.

She knew instinctively Gabrielle was His One. She had to stop this.

Gabrielle could hear people passing by in the corridor outside. The fear of being found out added to the excitement of being in his arms. They had to be quick because he was due to make his speech soon.

They composed themselves and left the room one at a time. She waited a few minutes before returning to the main room; checked herself in her mirror, trying to catch her breath.

She got back to her table just in time to hear him speak.

. . .

After dinner, everyone mingled and chit-chatted away; Gabrielle played her part and circulated the room, ensuring everyone was all right.

"He looks so handsome", she heard someone say. It was a group of women working in the head office from the communication department.

"I'm wondering who is he screwing now? Poor *Nathalie*", one of them said.

"I bet she lost count," they all nodded.

"I think he is seeing *la Directrice des Ressources Humaines* right now, or so I have heard," she added.

"I'm one of the other other other women," Gabrielle stood there incredulous.

He opened her up to sexual and emotional freedom she had never before experienced. But, despite his claims to her being the woman in his life, that did not imply she had been the only one either.

She wondered how many had been before — even worse if there was someone else now.

. . .

Le PDG suddenly appeared from right behind them. The four gossiping women looked partly in shock, mortified and, most of all, terrified. *Le PDG* had heard them. They disassembled and left with their tail between their legs.

Gabrielle noticed something else, though:
HE was the one looking terrified.

Not of what people were saying about him but of what Gabrielle was thinking. He could see it in her face. Her beautiful face was now turning away from him.

"Gabrielle, please don't leave," he said.

She couldn't bear to look at him and slowly but surely walked away. He could feel he was losing her right there.

They didn't talk for the rest of the evening. Then, finally, Gabrielle made her excuses and left early. The event team had everything under control, and no one needed her.
But him.

Right now, though, she didn't care. She returned to her hotel room and lay there, staring at the ceiling for hours. Her mobile phone was buzzing from the myriad of texts and voicemails he had left.

Gabrielle couldn't talk to him. Neither did she want to.

. . .

"What have I left myself into?" she thought.
"Why did I ...?

The next day was the conference's second day, and she would have called in sick if she could.

But she had commitments, so she put on a brave face and carried on as normally as possible. She avoided being in the same room alone with him as much as feasible.

Le PDG, on the other hand, wanted to be alone with Gabrielle.
Desperately.

He had to explain. Yes, there had been many before her. But they were just sex. There wasn't anybody else right now. There hadn't been anybody else since her.

Not since he first saw her, even before they had started being together.

He had to explain. Gabrielle had to know.

It was then when he wrote THE letter; he poured his heart and soul into paper.

".... All this madness I asked of you, I know there is confusion in your silence — but there are no actual words to describe my great love....

. . .

Last night I dreamed about you .... We kept fusing into one another. I was you. You were me.

... But you were a different, a shadow, as drawn with chalk, and you were lifeless, fading away from me.

Please don't leave me, my darling Gabrielle. I am nothing without you.

I'm yours forever."

"Yes, forever mine, forever hers," she thought at the time.

And now *Le PDG* was standing between her and the most amazingly perfect man she had ever met. Loving, open, available physically and emotionally, present and tender.

Now she was the one who had to explain to Mr Wonderful. Desperately.

"How to explain what *Le PDG* had meant to her and why?" she wasn't even sure she knew herself to the full extent.

One thing was for sure. He had to know there wasn't anybody else right now. And there hadn't been anybody else since him. Or ever will.

Me, myself and us.

" 'WHAT ARE YOU AFRAID OF?' HE ASKED.
'LOSING CONTROL.' I REPLIED.
'SOMETIMES LOSING CONTROL CAN BE WICKED AWESOME.' HE SAID.
' AND SOMETIMES IT'S A DISASTER.'""

- WORDSAREPUREMAGIC

FREEDOM OVER ME

THE NINE LIVES OF GABRIELLE: FOR THREE, SHE STRAYS

The Global annual meeting had ended; it had been an astounding success, especially for Gabrielle.

People commented on how different this year had been, more inclusive, more fitting of a multi-billion euros global company, a leader in its field, rather than a provincial French company. Tradition and heritage had the rightful place in the strategy.

Everybody appreciated the changes and felt the company was also starting to speak their language.

It was a bittersweet victory for Gabrielle, professionally elating but personally devastating.

Le PDG tried desperately to reach her, to talk to her. He had to explain. Gabrielle had to know.

"*Madame, pour Vous,*" the concierge said whilst she was checking out of the hotel and handed over a letter.

"*Merci,*" she said and settled the bill.

Looking at her handwritten name on the envelope, she knew it was from him. But she didn't open it whilst on the train back to Paris, too many people she knew around.

She was going back to London from there for a well-deserved long weekend; there, on the Eurostar, with a glass of some kind of liquor in her hand, she started reading:

. . .

"Dear Gabrielle,

Don't be afraid of how much I desire you. I will shield you with love the next time I see you, with kisses and caresses.
I want to dive with you in all the pleasures of the flesh so that you faint.
I want you to be astounded by me and admit that you have never dreamed of such things possible …………..."

Tears were streaming down her cheeks.
"…….You have raised new hope and fun in me, and I love you…."

"*Madame, are you OK?*" asked the attentive train server. They didn't often see many people crying their hearts out in business class.

"I'm good, thank you. Thanks for asking," Gabrielle replied.

"All this madness I asked of you, I know there is confusion in your silence — but there are no actual words to describe my great love…." she continued reading.

"Last night I dreamed about you …... I was you. You were me.

. . .

Then, we caught fire. I remember I was smothering the fire with my shirt. But you were different, a shadow, as drawn with chalk, and you were lifeless, fading away from me.

Please don't leave me, my darling Gabrielle. I am nothing without you.

I'm yours forever."

"Yes, forever mine, forever hers," she thought. It was the longest two and half hours of her life.

She spent the next twenty-four hours in bed. She couldn't be bothered doing anything or going anywhere. *Le PDG's* letter clutched in her hands.

Gabrielle was feeling both aching for him and repulsed at the same time.

She hadn't spoken to him yet. He called her numerous times, but she didn't pick up. She let the calls go to voicemail every time. He texted her a myriad of times, and she didn't respond either.

Ring, ring .... ring ring ...

Her mobile was buzzing.

. . .

"Ciao bella," the voice said "bentornata." It was Paola, her trusted friend, checking in on her.

"Hiya," Gabrielle replied. They chatted for a while, she really wanted to be left alone, but she knew her friend was trying to jerk her out of her apathy.

"Cicci, lunch on Sunday," Paola said.

It wasn't a question, and she wouldn't have taken no for an answer anyway.

"I'll come to Islington, and we'll go somewhere in your area."

Gabrielle knew it was pointless arguing or saying no; she would have shown up at her house anyway. Paola knew how to shake her up when she needed it.

"Remember to bring your passport when you are travelling from the suburbs," Gabrielle said, with their longstanding joke about Paola living in Richmond.

"I'll try. See you Sunday," she said.

Sunday came quicker than she realised, et voilà, it was soon time to meet Paola for a good catch-up.

Paola, her no-nonsense Italian friend who she had known since she had arrived in London.

Paola managed not to lose her strong accent after almost twenty years in the country. She always made Gabrielle smile.

The weather was warming up, and they were looking for somewhere to eat with outside space. Londoners turn into mini lizards and seek the sun whenever it seems like it is coming out.

Ultimately, they opted for The Alwyne Castle, a charming pub in Islington with a beer garden, situated only a minute's walk from Highbury & Islington underground station.

The Alwyne has lots of space, especially outside, which is ideal for building a suntan and carries a good beer and wine selection.

They met for an early Sunday lunch; Gabrielle definitely needed some cheering before heading back to Paris.

"Hello ladies," said the waiter "a table outside or inside?"
"Outside, outside," they replied in unison.

They both glanced at the menu and quickly chose: beef carpaccio and seared scallops, perfectly done and seasoned for starter and the obligatory Sunday Roast (obviously).

"Any drinks while you are waiting?"

Gabrielle and Paola looked at each other and said, "A bottle of house red and sparkling water, thanks."

. . .

"So, *ciccia mia*, what's going on?" Paola started as soon as the waiter had left their table.

It had been a while since they last saw each other, and they had a lot to talk about.

Gabrielle, slowly and softly, started to tell her story: her first meeting with *Le PDG*, their clandestine meetings anywhere and everywhere, and, to finish, she recounted what just happened in *Londrienne* at the global annual conference.

"Seared scallops?" the server interrupted.
  "Me," Paola raised her hand.

"*Ciccia, ciccia*, no, no, no ..." Paola went on after he had served them with their starters.

"But, but you are having an affair too," Gabrielle responded, baffled.

Paola had been married to an Englishman for the last ten years, and they had two gorgeous daughters. She loved them all dearly; however, she had kept her bit on the side: an Italian lover Paola met from time to time when visiting her mother every couple of months.

. . .

"*La differenza mia cara,* for me it's just sex.

I tell Marco I'm going over; if he is available, we meet; if he isn't, it is still OK, like a 'human vibrator' on call. Nothing else. He knows how to make me come, and he does his job.

He doesn't want or need anything more from me and me from him."

Her husband lacked a bit in the sex drive department and was happy to go without it. Paola wasn't.

Martin was an outstanding father and husband; she would never leave him, but needs were needs.

"*Tu ciccia mia,* are getting involved. No, correction, you are involved emotionally.

Plus, you feel guilty even when you find money on the pavement or someone gives you extra change in shops. Remember that time you went back to return ten pence? Ten pence. And now you are having an affair with a married man?" she paused, shaking her head.

"No, no, no, not for you. I can read guilt splattered all over your face; it is consuming you."

The main course arrived; Gabrielle was impressed that they managed to handle the timing of the two orders with no problem, especially considering she liked her beef still muuuing and rare whilst her friend liked it almost cremated.

The beef was delicious, and the beef-dripping roast potatoes were perfectly cooked.

. . .

Gabrielle knew Paola was right. But she couldn't bear to stop it yet.

"Relationships aren't easy," she thought, "they take a different take because the memories and stories can transform during crucial moments," she was illuding herself.

Finally, they ended the meal with the British Cheeseboard washed down with more red.

"*Se hai bisogno, lo sai che sono qui,*" Paola said.
    "I know."

At 6.00 am on Monday morning, Gabrielle started to get ready to leave the house. The first Eurostar to Paris was at 7.00 am, and St Pancras station was not that far from her home; she had plenty of time.

The two and a half hours seemed to pass by incredibly slowly. It felt more like a lifetime.
    On the one hand, she was glad. But, on the other hand, she wasn't really looking forward to seeing him again. Gabrielle was postponing the inevitable, and she had to meet him sometime. She was working directly for him, after all.

Until meeting *Le PDG*, Gabrielle's life experience was mainly secondhand, observed, and never viscerally involved. And now that her layers were slowly peeling away, and all the emotions she had repressed for so long, jealousy, frustration, and anger were coming to the surface.

All her life, she had been a closet bohemian. She always loved to live big, outrageously. Outside she was the perfect daughter and businesswoman but inside, she had always been Isadora Duncan.

She wanted a life outside the bell curve and to suck the marrow out of life. But she wanted people to like her too…

And so, she conformed.

Gabrielle arrived at the office after 11.00 am. People were still buzzing from the conference; she noticed *Le PDG* was not in.

"Good," she thought. She preferred it that away, at least today.

The day went by, and she had meetings back to back, so she had no time to think.

She left the office a bit late but decided to walk home anyway. Even though it was a bit far from *Tour Montparnasse* to the right behind *Gare Du Nord,* she needed the fresh air.

When she arrived at her building, he was standing there. *Le PDG.* He was holding a bouquet of purple hyacinths, and one single red rose.

. . .

"I'm sorry," he said. "I should have told you myself. I took for granted that you knew about the gossip mill like everyone else seems to.

"I can't stop thinking about you. Please don't leave me. I am nothing without you."

And there he was, standing right in front of the building entrance; she couldn't get in without acknowledging his presence one way or the other.

She didn't want to, but she was aching for him.

"There has been no other since I met you. Only you," he continued.

"Did you get my letter?" he asked. Gabrielle nodded.

And suddenly, they were making love in her apartment, on the floor, on the table, starving for each other. They stayed up all night; it was the first time he had stayed over.

And from then on, it became more regular. Le PDG was scared of losing Gabrielle and was trying his best to reassure her.

She wasn't one of the many other women, but the other woman, nevertheless.

. . .

Relationships aren't easy; they take a different take because of the memories and stories transformed during crucial moments.

Gabrielle had decided to stop commuting for a bit and fully experience Paris. At least for a while. She had to give Paris the attention and love it deserved.

"Paris is always a good idea," Audrey Hepburn said.

"Indeed, it is Audrey. Indeed it is." And even though summer in France meant a looooong holiday for the French who escaped to the coast or family house, it was worthed.

Gabrielle enjoyed walking around Paris and taking in the open-air architectural views, which were even more breathtaking with the sunshine.

"Summer brings out the best in Paris", she thought, "long days and nights when you can enjoy walking out and about, stunning views, sipping cocktails on terraces and dining al fresco."

Her Paris apartment was small and without outside space, but there were many gorgeous parks in Paris she could enjoy:
    big ones (*Bois de Vincennes, Bois de Boulogne, Buttes-Chaumont, Parc Floral, Parc de la Villette*),
    elegant ones (*Palais-Royal, Jardin du Luxembourg, Jardins des Plantes*),

and the in-between (*Parc Monceau, Parc Montsouris*).

All very charming and hosting various summer events that pair well with picnic time, and Gabrielle took full advantage of them.

Le PDG sometimes stayed at the weekend, and they relished watching the occasional movie in the *Parc de la Villette*, where there is a month-long *Cinema en Plein Air festival* with the city's most gigantic movie screen.

It was perfect, almost idyllic: some delicious food and a bottle of wine watching a movie whilst the sun set - the illusion of a proper relationship.

With or without *Le PDG* though, Gabrielle wanted to enjoy Paris, sometimes taking a tour alone from a boat on the Seine.

A tour on *Les Bateaux Mouches* lasts approximately two and six hours. It offers great sightseeing with commentary with plenty of Champagne. Or a meal served on exquisite white linen.

She deserved to experience all of it.

She loved how, in the summer, Paris becomes a seaside resort and welcomes *Paris Plages* in the new *Parc Rives de Seine*, with sun loungers and palm trees popping up just by the water's edge.

Plus, every boutique and department store in Paris has super anticipated sales *soldes d'été*.

She was squeezing in as much as she could as if she knew ...

Summer came and went, and the relationship with *Le PDG* became more stable, almost routine, and predictable.

It was as if they had sucked the marrow out, and now only the bones were left behind, holding the skeleton up. But nevertheless, he was still her addiction.

Gabrielle realised that she had now been in Paris, in her position, for almost a year.

"Career progression is slow in Paris," she had been thinking.
    "Somehow, people stay in the same position much longer than in the UK, where everyone expects to be promoted or move every couple of years".

She was feeling restless but wasn't quite sure why.

Her role kept her very busy with regular travel to the company's different branches worldwide. In addition, Christmas was just around the corner.

She was away from the office more and more, and working from home started to creep in from the London home.

· · ·

She started commuting again and travelling back on Thursdays more regularly.

And then, just like that, everything changed ...

On Monday, 23 March 2020, the Prime Minister announced the first lockdown in the UK, ordering people to stay home. And on 26 March, the lockdown measures legally came into force. Gabrielle was stuck in London.

Life can turn just in a second. Just like that. All the things you always wanted to do on pause. Until someone else decides to press the play button again.

Tomorrow, always longing for tomorrow, and suddenly, there almost wasn't a tomorrow.

Gabrielle kept in touch with the office, making great use of Teams and Zoom and continued working.

To be fair, she enjoyed being back in her home and the alone time.

She had always been a loner: a child lost in her books, as an adult chasing the next win in the never-ending climb.

She had cancelled many events before, dates, and meetings with friends at the last minute.

. . .

There was always tomorrow. There was always something more important to do.

But, after a while, her body and brain started fighting themselves. They were fighting her or something.

She felt exhausted all the time, and all the energy was wiped out of her. She was so fatigued that she struggled to complete even the most minor tasks. And yet, Gabrielle was unable to get any rest.

She tested to see if she had caught the dreaded C, but no, she hadn't.

Her body was on fire. And on top of throbbing soreness, she was experiencing pins-and-needles sensation prickling throughout.

Her mind went into overdrive to the point where she felt paranoid, irritable and moody. She couldn't stay still for even a moment.

She couldn't understand what was happening to her.

After a few months, with the physical symptoms subsiding, she started seeing things clearly again.

She had been withdrawing from the most potent drug.

. . .

Overall, the various lockdowns and consequent restrictions had been good for her, a time to focus on herself with little distraction.

And now, after the 'detox,' she was getting to know who Gabrielle actually was or wanted to be.
Fully and unapologetically. Isadora Duncan and all.
And levelling up big time.

The pandemic gave Gabrielle a new, more in-depth appreciation of being alone in gratitude for life. Appreciating everything that she was so lucky to be able to experience.

Sometimes it takes a great emergency or crisis to delve deep and discover how much more you can do. Or should do.

Gabrielle had never been afraid to make big choices: she left her big corporate job, Paris and *Le PDG*, in the middle of the pandemic.

Everybody thought she was crazy. But she knew it was the right thing to do.

She wanted to take her time to figure out what she really wanted. And so she reconnected with her inner Isadora, reprised some childhood passion, and started writing and illustrating children's books and a YouTube channel/ podcast.

. . .

She also began to treat her body and herself with more love and kindness, with no more torture and self-flagellation with super hard schedules. Or self-destructive affairs. Nothing left to prove.

She liked this Gabrielle. And this Gabrielle had attracted the most wonderful man.

She had to make sure that Mr Wonderful knew that THE letter he was holding in his hands was only a page in the book of her life, a chapter fully closed. She was waiting to continue writing her story with him and only him.

For Gabrielle had played, had strayed, and now she was ready to stay.

PART III

THE NINE LIVES OF GABRIELLE: FOR THREE, SHE STAYS

To London, one of my three loves.
Shh, don't tell anyone: you are my favourite!

LONDON CALLING

THE NINE LIVES OF GABRIELLE: FOR THREE, SHE STAYS

"**M**a Chérie Gabrielle,
    n'aie pas peur de combien je te désire."

The crumpled piece of paper he was holding was not ordinary paper. It was a letter. A letter to Gabrielle. In French. He could feel somehow that his day was about to change.

Funny how things can alter so quickly.

The day had started so well. The sun filtering through the gap in the heavy curtains woke them gently.

His arms were still around her; he found that he couldn't quite sleep without being close to her, skin-to-skin. As if he was scared, she was about to fly away.

Gabrielle was lying there, motionless, looking at him sweetly, her hair ruffled, cheeks flushed, trying not to breathe. Precious moments contemplating how lucky he was.

They were back home after a long weekend celebrating the day they met — he organised it as a surprise for her, together with an overnight stay at a central hotel. And then, they spent the previous day talking; well, for the first time, it was Gabrielle talking. About herself and why she had been so distracted, he had noticed but was not going to say anything. He knew how difficult it was for her to open up. But open up, she did; it must have been excruciating.

. . .

"Good morning", she purred and sunk her face into his chest without looking into his eyes. He knew she had done enough sharing, at least for now, far more than she was used to, so he held her firmly, stroking her back whilst kissing her forehead.

"I love you," Mr Wonderful whispered, "always" he felt he needed to reassure her. He wanted Gabrielle to know she could tell him anything.

"I love you too, more than I can say," she replied.

Mr Wonderful believed she was telling the truth. Emotional intimacy was not her forte. She was used to standing on her own two feet and relying only on herself, not showing her emotions. But there was more to her, he could sense it, and he was willing to uncover the depth of her, bit by bit.

Gabrielle told him about her impromptu adventure in New York, travelling alone after the break up of a long-term relationship, and how she explored the city, spending time alone, getting to know herself.

"She also managed to have a quick relationship," he found himself snarking as he recalled the story about the VP, the places they had been and so on.

"Am I being judgemental here?" perhaps he was a bit; he felt a sting, particularly when she mentioned how they had met. It was almost the same as they did: a chance encounter in the street quickly turned into something more. He thought theirs was unique and magical; he had never felt that instant connection and attraction.

Mr Wonderful was sure Gabrielle had said something about never accepting invitations from strangers; it had never happened to her before either.

"Well, looks like it kind of had," he admitted, disappointed.

They had stayed in bed lingering—the crumpled bed sheets around them. Then, finally, Gabrielle got up and got ready for her morning walk. Mr Wonderful was a gym-type of person, and she was not. God knows he tried to organise sports activities and exercise routines they could do together. But no, Gabrielle doesn't do exercise. And that was OK; they both needed their space.

Between falling deeply in love and lockdown, they practically moved in together almost immediately. However, he was wary of not 'overstepping' and being overfamiliar.

He needed to do some work and thought he would ask if he could use her office; Gabrielle was precious with her space, house, and things. She wasn't used to sharing. He had grown up with four other brothers in Brooklyn, so alone time or space had never been a real option.

"Bye, see you later," she said, closing the door behind her.

. . .

Mr Wonderful jumped out of bed and into a quick shower before getting ready to do some work. He made some fresh coffee and then proceeded towards the small crook in the corner of the house that Gabrielle had designated as her office. In this creative hub, she did all her work, painting, writing and filming for her YouTube channel for her new creative career. The house had clear areas dedicated to different activities; she had perfectly mixed old and new, period and modern. Everything was neat in its place, with clear boundaries and multipurpose. A foldable antique lacquered screen concealed the area from plain view.

He sat down, powered up his laptop, checked his emails, and then the stock exchange, followed by a quick call to his broker to sell and buy some stock and shares. He had left New York a few years back, tired of the hypocrisy of the Upper East side scene and running around trying to avoid the paparazzi. Instead, he loved London, its history, the pomp and ceremony and, most importantly, the fact that nobody knew or cared who he was. He could pop into a bookshop, and nobody batted an eyelid.

He had been coming regularly to the UK for the British Grand Prix at Silverstone and tennis at Wimbledon, and now he had made it home. London had been calling, and he had answered. He was here to stay.

The desk was ideally situated by the window, looking over Canonbury Square and Canonbury Gardens, perfect for peace and quiet but also for people-watching. However, he couldn't stop thinking about Gabrielle; he had never met anybody before who was this enchanting, enthralling, and so elusive. His previous long-term relationships had always played a second field to his business and personal interests: cars, racing, and flying. They simply couldn't hold his total attention. He had always been a very intense, single-minded person with a voracious sexual appetite and energy to spare. An all-or-nothing type of man and his all had not been love until now.

Now, all he wanted was Gabrielle. Her big brown eyes had captivated him from the first moment; her perfume seduced him, and her voice sealed the deal. But, most of all, it was her sweetness and vulnerability hiding behind the strong and badass facade. He had been careful not to scare her off with his intensity and had replaced his passion with old fashion romance and attentiveness in the hope of bringing down her barriers. He had acted like Prince Charming, trying to sweep her off her feet and win her over the old-fashioned way.

"Boy, I am in trouble," he felt it from the first time he saw her.

Mr Wonderful had been writing and checking emails for a while, but he now needed to print some documents. The printer was fully set up, but there wasn't enough paper for the file he needed to print.

"Where does she keep the paper for the printer?" he asked himself.

"Everything is so organised; it must be somewhere put neatly away. I am sure she has a place somewhere in here, hidden away from plain sight."

. . .

He started to open the drawers one by one. One quick peek at the time. He was surprised by what he found in some — a picture taken shortly after they had met — it seemed so far away like they had been together for a lifetime and yet so close. Everything was fresh, romantic and unaffected by the lockdown and the humdrum of ordinary life. Notebook after notebook. One for every imaginable task and hurdles of sketching pads with all designs and illustrations for the new children's book. But no printing paper.

One after the other, he looked into them all and then, finally, he found it. It had to be in the last one, obviously.

He took out enough paper to cover his needs when he saw something stuck at the back. He bent slightly and felt his way through the back of the drawers with his hand to pull it out. The piece of paper seemed stuck in between as it had yet to decide if it wanted to stay in the cabinet or come out. He was tempted to pull it out with force, but then he wasn't sure what it was, so he paid attention so as not to break it. When he finally managed to get it out, he realised it was a letter.

The handwriting pressed on the paper as if it had been written with haste or passion. He knew how private Gabrielle was and how long it had taken for her to open up. She only just told him about New York and her 'adventures' there.

So he left it be. Neatly resting on the desk. Mr Wonderful continued working for a while. But he couldn't concentrate; the letter was calling for him to open it. He was curious. He was tempted.

"A little peak," he thought, "and then I put it right back where I found it."

"I shouldn't look," reminding himself how private she was.

"I wonder if it is something she thinks is lost? Maybe she'll be glad I found it," he said, trying to find a reason to go ahead.

That little piece of paper did not stop bating him; like a siren luring sailors to rocky shores, it kept calling and tempting him to open it and read it. For hours he resisted and kept on working, keeping busy. But he couldn't concentrate; he was too distracted.

The letter kept popping into his mind. Then, finally, he gave in; he made another cup of coffee, sat down and unfolded the inviting note. And so he carefully, slowly unfolded the paper, a door to a secret world and started reading:

"*Ma chérie Gabrielle, n'aie pas peur de combien je te désire.*"

"Brilliant! In French," how ironic "I find a new way in, and there is extra 'security'," he smiled.

Mr Wonderful French was rusty, but he could comprehend a few words here and there like "*désire.*"

· · ·

He understood it was a letter to Gabrielle rather than from Gabrielle and from someone who knew her, from what he remembered from his school days. Mr Wonderful glanced further, but his schoolboy French was essential, too basic to comprehend everything fully but enough to understand the gist of it.

He looked up Google Translate on his laptop and started typing the letter, line by line. For some reason, he was nervous. He typed word by word carefully. He wasn't quite sure he should. He shouldn't have. It would have been better if he hadn't.

But he did.

"Dear Gabrielle, don't be afraid of how much I desire you,"

read the first line. He felt uncomfortable somehow; reading someone else's letter didn't feel right, even though he was curious.

"Who writes handwritten letters anymore?" he asked himself and cursed himself for not paying more attention to the French classes in school and not practising more French with Gabrielle.

The process of typing and translating phrase by phrase was excruciatingly painful. So slow.

I will shield you with love the next time I see you, with kisses and caresses.

I want to dive with you in all the pleasures of the flesh so that you faint.

"Flesh ... faint. Who does he think he is?"

I want you .... to be astounded by me and admit .... that you have never dreamed of such things possible …

"Astounded," he mocked.

... And then, when you are old, I want you to remember and tremble with pleasure when you think of me...

"Tremble with pleasure," he repeated "the man is trying hard; I can't blame him for that," Mr Wonderful thought. Then, however, his heart started sinking a little, and his mind started playing games.

You make me hotter than hell ... everything you do gets me hotter than hell.

"Shit, very expressive" his throat was dry.

You have raised new hope and fun in me, and I love you; your pussy hair I felt with my fingers,

"What the f**k?" Mr Wonderful felt the words like daggers to his heart when it finally realised it wasn't a letter of unrequited love, a proposal ...

I felt the inside of your pussy, hot and wet with my fingers...

He had never sworn or used explicit words with her, and she never looked comfortable when he played with her, always holding back. Always on the verge of orgasm but not quite letting go.

• • •

All this madness I asked of you, I know there is confusion in your silence — but there are no actual words to describe my great love....

My Wonderful had to stop; tears were streaming down his cheeks, blurring his vision. He hadn't cried since his mother died and couldn't remember a time he did before or after that, and he couldn't understand why now.

He stood up and went to make himself another cup of strong coffee. A needed distraction. A delay tactic. The kettle took what felt like ages to boil. Minutes went by like hours. He was pacing the small kitchen. Fear and anger replaced sadness and hurt and then back again.

He couldn't believe she was keeping this type of secret. She told him no more after their talk.

Shhhhh ... whiiiiiiieeee ...

The kettle, finally, whistled. Pouring the water slowly had little or no calming effect on him.

"Has she been seeing someone else? Is she still seeing someone else? Is she ending it?"

All sorts of scenarios were going through his head, and his fears and doubts completely overtook logic and common sense.

. . .

"No, can't be. Gabrielle wouldn't have an affair. She couldn't have," he thought. "At least physically," reason starting to kick in, if only for a moment.

"Maybe it was before New York ..." recalling she had been vague about that relationship.

"No, it can't be." Gabrielle sounded peeved about it when she mentioned it, "Wouldn't have kept the letter for so long", Mr Wonderful concluded.

"Have they been talking? Emailing? Face-timing? She must have." The running commentary in his head was driving him crazy with doubt.

Mr Wonderful sat at the desk again. The letter was there, waiting and bating him still.

Last night I dreamed about you; I do not know what occurred explicitly. What I do know is that we kept fusing into one another. I was you. You were me.

Then, we caught fire. I remember I was smothering the fire with my shirt. But you were different, a shadow, as drawn with chalk, and you were lifeless, fading away from me.

Please don't leave me, my darling Gabrielle. I am nothing without you. xxx"

. . .

No signature, no name. It wasn't needed. She knew.

He read it and re-read it repeatedly, and then the translation. And again, and the translation. Checking he had typed each word correctly into Google.

"One of two words can change everything …."

There was no date. He had yet to find an envelope for it. But the letter was somehow 'lived'; there were marks, stains, and perhaps the slight tinge of her mascara...

He imagined her tears falling onto the paper and tried deciphering a timeline. But he couldn't, no matter how much he tried.

"She has a lot of meetings. She always takes phone calls in private. Was he at the 'meetings'?" His mind was now a runaway train.

Every time the phone rang, she seemed jumpy and took the calls away from him to another room. Her phone was always with her, texting and scrolling.

"Was she talking to him?"

Suddenly everything felt so confusing.

. . .

"Her aloofness was making sense now," he concluded, a sign he had disregarded.

"Where is she now? Did she go to meet him?" he couldn't help wondering.

"This is an awfully long walk," then thought.

"I should go back home now," Gabrielle was thinking simultaneously, but she was enjoying her stroll.

Gabrielle always loved walking and even more so during the various lockdowns. With Mr Wonderful living with her, it was one way to carve some time for herself without hurting his feelings.

She always wanted an all-consuming, passionate kind of love, the 'you-can't-live-without-each-other' type. Still, she had yet to quite realise what it meant in practice, being in each other's pockets twenty-four-seven. Or worse, intimacy.

So Mr Wonderful had his gym time, and Gabrielle had her walks.

She used to walk a lot by the seaside when she was little. The little village felt claustrophobic, but she always felt free by the ocean. Gabrielle loved the ocean, the sea, its temper, its moods, and the sheer grandeur. She always imagined the treasures hiding beneath, sunken ships bringing gold and jewels, people buried at sea and all the creatures who lived there. She loved watching the waves come to shore and the seagulls flying low.

Squawk, squawk ... squawk ...

She loved absorbing every bit of the sounds and the smell. So now she walked by the canal instead. She went there as much as she could. Watching the boats moving slowly, the seagulls passing by. It was her way to find peace and connect with whatever 'something' was out there.

Sometimes she took longer when she felt like she was losing herself. But one thing was for sure: Gabrielle didn't want Mr Wonderful to feel she regretted moving in together or missed anything or anyone from her past. She didn't, really.

Gabrielle had permanently and firmly closed each door behind her. Her exes were totally and genuinely exes.

Only *Le PDG* had lingered longer than necessary. He had been contacting her from time to time, trying to win his way back in.

With him, she rediscovered her wilder, freer self, the passionate, inhibited side hidden for so long, her unquenched sexuality and her first orgasm, a part of herself that had been suitably reined in. But she had also found a part of herself she didn't like at all.

. . .

Gabrielle was scared now; she felt like a dormant and active volcano that may erupt at any time and cause dangerous earthquakes and mudslides.

Lockdowns had been a blessing in disguise for her when Gabrielle's healing journey began. She stepped out of the craze of always seeking someone new and instead always meeting the same old sad, lonely child; herself. She knew she could not outrun it. So she turned within and was happy for now with a gentler, more romantic love until she had found strength. Mr Wonderful was her knight in shining armour. Her Saviour.

"I wonder what Mr Wonderful is working on this morning? Stock, shares, buying a new company?" Gabrielle pondered.

She had fitted the corner of her house as an office/creative space since she had started her new career as a creative. All her drawings, mood boards, and manuscripts were neatly arranged in their place, ready for use but away from prying eyes.

Mr Wonderful had asked politely if he could use the space; he usually sits on the sofa with his laptop resting on his legs to check his emails and take calls.

She always felt that was her space, her creative 'cave'.

. . .

"What's wrong with that?" she thought. "I suppose when you live with someone, you need to share a little," trying to convince herself.

Gabrielle wasn't used to sharing. An only child, she had only ever lived briefly with someone once before. And she never quite used to it. The sharing. Opening up.

"Time to go home," she said, returning to the townhouse in Canonbury Square.

Her neighbours were returning from their walk or whatever they'd been doing. They became 'close' during the lockdown, the whole square serving as an extended pretend bubble. Gabrielle had bought the house one year earlier and didn't know anybody before the pandemic. But the community spirit kicked in on full blast during the pandemic. In between the NHS clapping, they got to 'know' and support one another and even organised regular Friday night 'drink up' zoom calls with games. It was her place, the place she worked herself up to have for so long before events changed everything—Paris and then the big C. She could never bring herself to say the full word aloud, didn't want to speak it into existence even more, at least not in her existence.

Gabrielle turned the key and opened the door. She closed it behind her slowly, still absorbed in her thoughts. She walked around the ground floor, but Mr Wonderful was nowhere to be seen.

.   .   .

"Perhaps he is still working upstairs," she thought. She could smell fresh coffee coming from the kitchen. She took a long breath in "*Sniff .... sniff ...*' and inhaled '*Mmm ...* '

She worked her way up the stairs to the corner study on the first floor. She was tired; it had been a draining few days. All that talking about herself was not something she was used to. Nevertheless, she felt she had to after the Opera. She had been absent-minded, with her memories taking her back and forward, shifting realities.

And Mr Wonderful had been so, of course, wonderful, thoughtful and caring. He deserved more.

And so, for the first time, Gabrielle told him about her solo adventure in New York, wandering the city, meeting the VP and their brief affair. Well, she glossed a little over the affair. She loved the idolised version of herself she could see reflecting in his eyes and didn't want to ruin it. Instead, Gabrielle wanted him to understand the sense of freedom she had experienced. Freedom and independence were important to her. Or at least the beginning of her freedom journey.

Gabrielle had omitted that she had also been running around New York searching for a fantasy figure, Goren. That would have sounded too crazy to understand. Stalking a TV character and his incarnation was too much to share and comprehend. Heck, she didn't understand it either.

. . .

Mr Wonderful listened patiently and attentively and asked a few questions here and there but was delicate enough to stop when he sensed she was uncomfortable.

"Thank God," she thought.

Gabrielle was always uncomfortable sharing too much; if she didn't have to, she preferred not to.

She was feeling mentally and emotionally exhausted, but she loved him. Mr Wonderful was well and truly incredible. And patient. Always listening. Somehow she thought he was waiting for something ...

She knew she could tell him everything, and he wouldn't judge. Everything but Paris. Not Paris.

Mr Wonderful was a man of principle with a strong moral compass, and she was scared she'd lose him. His father had many affairs and left his mother to fetch for herself and five boys. This was one of those times when the entire story was better left unsaid.

"Where is he?" she wondered, going up the stairs.

She had created a little piece of heaven in the corner with her books, her YouTube set and the desk she inherited from her French grandmother. *Mamé* always encouraged her artistic tendencies. During her summer visits, they used to walk by the sea together and then stop and paint. She wished she had spent more time with her in recent years. But, unfortunately, she was always too busy travelling. Working.

"I'll go next month," she always told herself. But the 'next month' never came.

"Oh, there he is" she saw him sitting in front of the desk.

Mr Wonderful was slouching on the chair, a letter clenched in his hands, a throbbing wrinkle on his forehead. He looked pale. He lifted his head, and then she saw. His face was tinging on grey, his eyes red and swollen as if he had been crying.

He realised too he was not alone anymore. Gabrielle was back home and standing right there in front of him, looking at him intensely with her big brown eyes, squinting a little. She was always doing that when she was thinking. Her cheeks were slightly flushed from her walk. Or perhaps they were flushed from the embarrassment of seeing him with the letter. Or guilt of being found out??!

"God, did it show he had been crying? Could she see?" He had wiped away the tears, but his eyes were still stinging.

He could feel his jaw tightening whilst his heart was beating faster, his palms sweaty. Gabrielle's hair was a little messy.

. . .

"What has she been doing?" imagining all sorts of things.

"What happened?" she thought. The way he looked at her sent shivers down her spine.

And then she saw the last drawer open. The drawer where she kept THE letter. The letter from *Le PDG*. Paris was still haunting her.

All her life, she had always taken the moral high ground on people having affairs, secretly disapproving of her friend Paola and her extra-marital sex on tap. A mix of her strict Catholic upbringing and *'le cadre'*, the ever-present rules with what's right and what's wrong clearly defined.

But in Paris, the lines blurred, and she found herself caged and chained to him, *Le PDG*, forgetting even common sense. And now Mr Wonderful had seen that letter.

"No, he didn't read it. He wouldn't."
    "Stupid, he has got it in his hands."

Gabrielle was trying to search through the chambers of her memory. Still, she couldn't remember how many or which of the lurid details were mentioned.

"But he doesn't speak French."

. . .

"Have you heard of Google, the internet, duh!"

"It's in the past; it's gone," she thought. "And how does he know that?" her alter ego intervened.

"Damn, I don't think there isn't a date in the letter," Gabrielle recalled.

"Oh God, he has been crying," she noticed. "He understands the letter ... "

"Does he think it's happening now???"

"What am I going to say? Should I say something?" thinking, thinking ...

"Perhaps I can pretend nothing happened; I haven't done anything. After all, I don't really know; something else might have happened."

"Yeah, right," the bitchy alter ego dropped in.

"Wait, he hasn't said anything yet. No hello, no darling," she realised.

He was sitting there, motionless and speechless.

. . .

"What is he thinking? Is he going to say something?"

"Why isn't he screaming at me? Ask me something?"

The silence seemed to go on forever, every second steeped in fear and sweat.

Time stood still.

Neither moved. Neither said a word.

He was looking at her; she was looking at him for what seemed like an eternity.

Mr Wonderful wanted to ask Gabrielle so many questions.

"Who is he? When did it end? Has it ended? Why did she end it? Or thinking about ending it? What does he have that he doesn't?"

He had never seen Gabrielle's more carnal and sensual side, not the one transpiring from the letter, and he wondered why not. Maybe it was his fault.

. . .

"Have I been too chivalrous? Too Hallmark romantic?"

They had sex daily, but it was soft, gentle, tender, almost pure. Mr Wonderful realised he had put her on a pedestal, idolised her and had been too patient with her, making excuses for her, scared to lose her.

"Yes, he was going to ask her," he concluded.

"What if she said she was still seeing him somehow? What would he do?" he was sweating now.

The thought of not being with her made him feel sick. He couldn't stay, but he knew he couldn't leave either. So perhaps he should say nothing. Ask nothing for now. Wait for her to approach the subject if she ever did.

She was biting her lips nervously, which she did when pondering what bothered her.

"Is she about to say something? What if she is angry? Angry that he went through 'her stuff' and pried. He found something about her before she was ready to open up about it."

Her right hand was clenched around the strap of her handbag, her knuckles had turned white, and her right foot was slightly tapping. Mr Wonderful was looking for signs of what to do next.

· · ·

Ring ring … ring ring …

His eyes flickered.

"Why isn't he answering his phone? Do something," she thought. He was looking at her.

"Oh wait, it's MY phone," she realised. Gabrielle searched for her mobile in her handbag, still draping from her shoulder.

"Why can't I ever find things quickly when I need them "... Lipstick, pens, notebook, sunglasses.

Ring ring …

"Where is the fr...ing phone?" There it is, at the bottom, of course.

"Hello Paola," she answered, looking at Mr Wonderful looking at her.

Gabrielle felt she had to make sure he knew who was calling. Just in case. The conversation went on for a couple of minutes.

"Let me check," she said. "Paola is asking if we'd like to go to dinner tonight, the last barbie of the season," she said, looking at Mr Wonderful. "Martin is cooking."

"Sure," he answered, surprising himself.

"What time do you want us there?" Gabrielle asked on the phone.

"Seven," she said with a questioning tone directed at Mr Wonderful. He nodded.

"OK, seven is good for us," she said to Paola. Gabrielle would have loved talking to her friend for longer, in private, but this was definitely not the right time.

In the end, she mustered up the courage to speak.

"Did you manage to do your work?" Gabrielle asked, her soft voice shaking.

"Yes, thank you," he replied faintly.

"Good walk?" he asked in return.

"Yes, thank you. I'm going to jump in the shower," she followed.

. . .

"OK," he replied, and for the first time ever, he didn't mention jumping in the shower with her.

"I need to pop out," he added.

'Sure, I need to work anyway."

"OK."

Gabrielle turned and went into the bathroom to re-compose herself. She closed the door behind her and locked the door for the first time in a long time.

"God, I look like I feel," she said, scrutinising herself in the mirror.

She looked like a mess: her hair was all over the place, red-faced. And then she realised Mr Wonderful didn't stand to greet her, nor did he kiss her. He always kissed her before she left the house or when they were going to be apart, and when she came back, from anywhere. No matter how little or long she had been away.

"He didn't kiss me," she repeated to herself.

Finally, after what seemed like a lifetime, she came out of the shower: she had scrubbed so much that she looked like a tomato.

. . .

Gabrielle started re-composing herself and dressed up with her working loungewear, but she couldn't quite bring herself to come out of the bathroom.

She pressed her hand and ear against the door, trying to understand if he was still there. Gabrielle didn't hear him going out, and right now, she couldn't hear a thing. Not a sound. She wasn't ready to be confronted and speak to him. Perhaps she could avoid him at least until it was time to go to Paola's. She didn't know what to say. There wasn't really much to say. *Le PDG* had been well and truly over for a year despite his attempts at reconciliation. But nevertheless, she realised that it was more than that.

Her ear was hurting now. She was pressing so hard. Not a squick. She finally decided it was time to go out and face the music. Gabrielle walked slowly, almost on tiptoes, turning around each corner with trepidation. Mr Wonderful had left the building. Suddenly she felt the need to rush to her desk.

"Where is the letter?"

There was no sign of it on the desk; she jam-slammed the drawer open. No, it was not there.

"Oh God, has he kept it?" she said. "He has kept it," she repeated over and over.

. . .

Le PDG wrote that letter to her when he feared Gabrielle was about to stop their affair and now was standing between her and the most amazingly perfect man she had ever met.

"How can I explain what *Le PDG* meant to me and why?" she wasn't even sure she knew herself to the full extent.

One thing was for sure. Gabrielle desperately wanted Mr Wonderful to know; he had to know there wasn't anybody else right now. And there hadn't been anybody else since him.

Beep beep beep …

A calendar notification.

"Sugar, I forgot" she had a zoom call scheduled with her virtual assistant to talk about her calendar, the cover for her new children's book and interviews for her podcast. It was precisely what she needed, some activity not to think about what had just happened.

For the first time, she couldn't be bothered to put her 'face on' and decided to stay as she was, just reading her notes and preparing for the meeting. The call came and went.

Still hours before dinner at Paola's and no sign of Mr Wonderful.

. . .

"Perhaps it's better this way." At least for now.

Gabrielle reflected on how refreshed she felt after the New York sabbatical, with a new outlook on life; she had thoroughly worked on herself and done some introspection. Or at least was she capable of at the time.

She found out she had so many shields and layers that she struggled to penetrate them herself. She had caged herself in—a self-imposed cage.

All her life, she had been a closet bohemian. She always loved to live big, outrageously. Outside she was the perfect daughter and businesswoman but inside, she had always been Isadora Duncan. She wanted a life outside the bell curve and to suck the marrow out of life.

But she wanted people to like her too... And so she conformed. So much so that she had lost herself.

And then Paris came. After the New York trip, it promised more freedom.

With *Le PDG*, Gabrielle became viscerally involved for the first time, a glimpse of herself. All the emotions, passion, capacity for creative self-expression, and everything she had repressed for so long came to the surface together with their darker counterpart: jealousy, anger, frustration and obsession.

· · ·

And in the process, she broke her values to meet her needs and got lost in the intensity of it.

Freedom was not freedom at all. Most importantly, she had deviated from her moral compass. Isadora or not.

But London started calling her back.

Ultimately, you can't run from yourself, but there is always one place you can call home where you are at most peace and alive.

Gabrielle always loved London. Its anonymity, its modernity, the unconventional and the weird. History and avant-garde, tradition and modernness. The tolerance of religions and races. She missed the more relaxed lifestyle and multiculturalism London provides, the general politeness and lack of judgement, including sartorial standards. You could go out in pyjamas, nobody cares.

London called her when she was younger and called her back when she needed it most.

Her stay in Paris concluded fairly uneventfully; Gabrielle started being away from the Paris office more and more, working from home. From the London home. Weekends were extended to Tuesdays and started on Thursdays.

. . .

The office didn't notice as she was usually travelling anyway. The only one who did was *Le PDG*. Their meetings became more and more infrequent. She just couldn't be in his presence. Their magnetism was far too strong and overpowering. She couldn't control herself when with him.

London was calling to write the next chapter of her life.

Then the pandemic happened, and luck struck to release her from his stronghold.

Gabrielle has played, has strayed and now she was ready to find herself again. So she left her corporate job and started a new creative career that gave her an outlet for all the passion bubbling beneath the surface.

Still wary, though, of unleashing Isadora fully, scared of what she was capable of doing. At least for now.

She could see herself with him. She was ready.

"God, where has the afternoon gone?" she said, but there was still no sign of Mr Wonderful.

"Where is he?" She was both worried for him and panicking.

"What if he doesn't come back?"

. . .

They should really leave for Paola's soon.

"It will take some time to reach South London with rush hour traffic," she thought, looking at her watch. But she was ready and waiting.

Mr Wonderful glanced at his watch.

"I should really go back," but he didn't feel like making the journey from Belgravia to Islington and then again to Richmond with Gabrielle, alone in the car, attempting to make small talk. Not right now.

He had spent the afternoon in his house in Eaton Square. He hadn't been there for months now.

He still remembered the thrill of buying the seven-bedroom, seven-bathroom Regency house from a disgraced hedge fund manager at a bargain price. Mr Wonderful loved the elegant garden squares and terraces of white stucco-fronted houses with pillared porches and black wrought-iron detailing, quintessentially English with quiet, traditional streets and a discreet feel. It was as if he had never left; the staff had kept it going as usual.

But today, the house felt cold. He was shivering.

. . .

He had kept the letter. Re-read it. Trying to rationalise. He was angry, most of all with himself.

He had showered, changed and gotten ready.

"I'm at mine. I'm going straight to Paola's from here. I'll wait for you outside so we can go in together," he texted.

Beep beep ...

Gabrielle recognised the ringtone straight away. It was Mr Wonderful.

"What? Shit," reading the text. "At least he is coming and talking to me ... kind of."

She ordered an Uber and waited. The car journey seemed longer than usual.

When the Uber stopped in front of Paola's, Mr Wonderful was just getting out of the car.

"Don't wait for me," he told his driver.

"Hi," she said.

· · ·

"Hi," he replied.

He was wearing the silk navy blue shirt she bought for him with dark jeans. It made his blue eyes glisten more. She could smell *Dior Homme.*

Mr Wonderful had brought flowers for Paola, burnt-coloured roses and sunflowers, and a couple of Martin's favourite bottles of red Malbec.

"Thank God he did," Gabrielle thought; she had forgotten entirely.

Gabrielle was wearing his favourite dress; she hoped he noticed.

"You look nice," he said. He couldn't help it; she did.

"Thank you," she replied with a faint smile.

"Was this a sign?" she was pondering, but Paola appeared at the door before she could say anything.

"Ciao bellissimi," and hug them both.

"My favourites," she said, accepting the flowers from Mr Wonderful.

. . .

"Che bella camicia caro," Paola added.

"Thank you," flashing one of his dazzling smiles. "You look gorgeous as usual."

"Parole, parole … Venite, venite," welcoming them in.

Martin had reached the door too now. Mr Wonderful waited for Gabrielle to enter, holding the door for her.

"See Micio, that's how it is done," Paola pointed to her husband.

"Stop making me look bad," Martin said, laughing and greeting Mr Wonderful, the two men chatting away.

"Come, Gabri, help me with the salad," Paola said. "Let the boys look after the barbie."

"Sure."

"What's wrong?" she asked as soon as they were out of sight. Apparently, her face was an open book.

. . .

Gabrielle quickly went through the day's events, checking over her shoulder from time to time.

"Ciccia mia," and then Paola gave her a big hug. No, I told you so; no comments or recrimination—just a big warm hug.

"Let's have some fun tonight and see if we can oil things a bit," Paola said.

" To conquer oneself is the best
and noblest victory;
to be vanquished by one's own nature is
the worst and most ignoble defeat"

\- PLATO

BACK IN YOUR ARMS

THE NINE LIVES OF GABRIELLE: FOR THREE, SHE STAYS

M r Wonderful and Gabrielle arrived separately for dinner at Paola's house, a Georgian property overlooking the duck pond in the quiet village of Ham, upstream of Richmond.

He was conscious of not embarrassing Gabrielle in front of her friends even though, most likely, he was sure the two women would speak about what had happened at some point.

But for tonight, he wanted to leave the events of the past twenty-four hours behind them and enjoy the evening. He liked them both, Paola and Martin.

"Interesting couple," he thought when he was first introduced to them.

A fiery Italian woman and a very, very Englishman couldn't have been more different if they tried. But they worked. Paola was a hot shot Chief Operating Officer for some global conglomerate, always travelling, and Martin, a Chief Financial Officer for a UK-based charity.

Gabrielle had known Paola for years through their work and had kept in touch ever since.

"Don't wait for me," he told his driver.

"Hi," she said.

. . .

She greeted him as he got out of the car; she looked so good, wearing his favoured dress, and he secretly hoped it was for him. A gesture.

He, too, had made an effort and wore the shirt she had got him as a present and her favourite perfume.

"Hi," he replied.

Mr Wonderful had brought flowers for Paola, burnt-coloured roses and sunflowers, and a couple of Martin's favourite bottles of red Malbec. His secretary kept a record of all the people he met, personally and for business, and what they liked: places, events, and things and normally took care of everything.

But this, he remembered himself.

Everything to do with Gabrielle and what she cared about was indelibly impressed in his memory.

Paola was as welcoming and warm as usual, greeting them with a hug.

"Ciao bellissimi," she said.

"My favourites," she said, accepting the flowers.
    "Che bella camicia caro," then added.

. . .

Martin was there too to welcome them.

As Mr Wonderful waited for Gabrielle to enter, holding the door for her, Paola jokingly said to her husband, "See Micio, that's how it is done."

"Stop making me look bad," Martin said, laughing and greeting Mr Wonderful, the two men chatting away.

Mr Wonderful and Gabrielle tried to act naturally, neither wanting to involve their friends in their trouble, both secretly wondering how the evening would pan out.

"Come, Gabri, come with me in the kitchen," Paola declared. "Let the boys look after the barbie outside."

Martin and Mr Wonderful went out and opened a couple of bottles of beer whilst getting ready for the barbecue. It was a nice but chilly evening, and the patio heater was switched on. They were eating on the open veranda, making the most of probably the last usable day of late autumn.

Paola knew something was bubbling out and blurted out, "What's wrong?" as soon as they were out of sight in the kitchen.

. . .

Gabrielle thought she had managed to hide the insecurity she was feeling right now, but apparently, she had not. She recounted the day's events, checking over her shoulder from time to time.

Paola was boisterous and loud but knew exactly what to do and when "Ciccia mia," she said and gave her a big hug. No, I told you so; no comments or recrimination—just a big warm hug.

"Let's have some fun tonight and see if we can oil things a bit," Paola said.

Paola put the flowers in a vase centre stage "Che belli," she said, smiling.

The table was overflowing with food: assorted Italian antipasti and prawn skewers, spatchcock chickens, coleslaw, and salad, all washed down with plenty of wine, white and red.

The conversation was flowing, and they chit-chatted about all sorts of topics. Mr Wonderful and Gabrielle were sitting across each other, furtively glancing at each other from time to time.

"Come and help me with the dessert Gabri," said Paola.

"Trouble in paradise?" Martin asked as the two women disappeared inside.

· · ·

Mr Wonderful turned to look at Martin, surprised.

"Well, the two of you are always all touchy-feeling all the time, and tonight you are ... hem .. just... 'friendly'. Is everything OK?"

He was about to answer when they heard, "Guys ... shall we close the doors and move inside? It's getting cold now outside," Paola asked, peeking through.

They looked at each other, started moving things around to close the french doors, and turned off the patio heater outside.

Paola served the tiramisu and more wine in the sitting room, where large colourful plump sofas were arranged to create a cosy and welcoming area. It was a place to slouch in comfort, English country shabby chic-like.

Tiramisu and more wine were followed by brandy, coffee, and more brandy until they all slouched and fell asleep.

Gabrielle woke up, the first light of the morning caressing her face. Her head rested on Mr Wonderful's chest, his arm around her. She couldn't remember how they got that way but was glad they did.

She looked around and saw Martin sleeping on the armchair, his head tilted backwards, snoring with his mouth open. Paola was already up.

"Shhhh," she whispered, pointing at the two men still sleeping.

"What a night!"

"Thank you!" Gabrielle said, getting off the sofa.

"No problem, Ciccia," Paola said, rushing around and trying to get ready.

"I need to jump in the shower. I have an early meeting," she added softly. "You can use the spare bathroom if you want to shower," she added.

"No, it's OK. I need to go back home and change. I have an interview this morning," Gabrielle said whilst looking at Mr Wonderful, who was still asleep.

"Don't worry," Paola said, "Martin will look after him. Just text him."

Gabrielle nodded, picking up some of the glasses still on the table.

. . .

"What are you doing? Leave it, leave it. The boys can take care of it; Martin is off work today. Have you thought about what you are going to do?"

"Not yet," Gabrielle answered.

"Well, let me know if you need anything. Call me if you need to talk."

"Thank you," Gabrielle said as she hugged Paola on her way out of the house.

"Good morning, sunshine; how are you?" Martin asked as Mr Wonderful was waking up and stretching on the sofa. A couple of hours had passed since the two women left the house.

"Morning," he replied. "OK, I think. How much did we have to drink?" he asked while looking around.

Martin waved his hand, pointing at the many empty bottles and glasses on the table. "A lot," he said.

"The girls have gone out already," Martin added. "Both have meetings this morning," Martin said, reading a note from Paola, realising he was looking for Gabrielle.

Mr Wonderful checked his phone and saw a text from her:

I need to go back home and change. Have an interview this morning. See you back at the house later? G xx

"Coffee?"

"I need a shower first," he said, holding his forehead "please," Mr Wonderful asked.

"Sure," Martin replied as he started collecting the empty bottles and glasses. "There are fresh towels in the spare bathroom you can use."

"Thank you. Let me give you a hand tidying up first."

After they both had showered and had some coffee, Martin said, "Let's go out for breakfast. We both need some fresh air."

"Want to talk?" he asked as they left the house.

There was a chill in the air; Mr Wonderful nodded, shivering, still wearing his silk shirt.

"Brrr ... Let's go to this cafe," Martin declared. "Too chilly to walk."

. . .

They sat down, and both ordered a full English. Somehow the boozing and abundance of food from the previous evening had made them both hungry.

"So, you want to talk about what's up?"

Mr Wonderful was reluctant to open up. But nonetheless, he needed to get everything off his chest and someone else's perspective. So he proceeded to describe the previous day's events: finding the letter, reading it, his doubts about the relationship, Gabrielle coming back home and then hiding in the shower.

Martin listened attentively, and then he said with his English aplomb, "So nothing happened then …"

Mr Wonderful looked at him, surprised.

"I mean, you didn't have a fight. You didn't catch her "*in flagrante*" or something of the sort."

"Well, no. No," he protested.

"You just found a letter from a lover. OK, a passionate lover, I'll give you that."

. . .

"Yes, but …" when he heard the summary of the day so simply put by Martin, he felt silly.

"Have I been massively overreacting?" he thought.

"The letter could have been from a present lover, but how likely is that? You two have been together twenty-four-seven since you met."

Mr Wonderful realised how stupid he had been when Martin asked, "What if she is? What if she is actually having an affair? What would you do?"

"I couldn't possibly stay …."

"Do you love her?" he pressed.

"She is the love of my life," the words just came out of his mouth.

"Then, what's the problem?"

Mr Wonderful could not believe he had just heard that comment when suddenly Martin blurted out, "Paola is having an affair" he paused, "Well, regular sex with someone, to be specific."

"Paola is a very passionate woman," he continued. "I've never been 'that way' inclined. All I ever wanted was a companion, a family. She is an amazing mother and a good wife. We have a great life: she has her career, and I have my family. And I could never leave my girls."

Mr Wonderful did not know what to say at this point. The man had a look of resigned acceptance on his face. He recognised that perhaps Martin needed to talk as much as he did, if not more.

"And you are OK with that?" he asked, realising he had a disbelieving look on his face when Martin responded, "Not exactly, but I have learnt to live with it. She is careful."

"Have the two of you talked about this?"

"Oh no, of course not. She doesn't think I know. I found out by chance." He took a bite of his breakfast and a sip of tea. "A text. From him. He would meet her at the airport."

Paola travelled back to Italy every few months for a long weekend to visit her sickly mother, and then they would meet if it worked for both of them. Drinks, sex until the next time.

Mr Wonderful was speechless. He had contemplated what he'd do if it turned out that Gabrielle was indeed having an affair. He knew he wouldn't want to be without her. But the thought of another man kissing her, touching her, or worse, being inside her when they were intimate made his stomach churn.

· · ·

"You have to decide what's more important to you. For me, it's my family. And I do love her. But I know I cannot give her what she needs," Martin stated.

"I get YOUR point," Mr Wonderful said, sipping his strong coffee. "But, you see, the woman described in the letter was not *my* Gabrielle; I didn't recognise her …."

"And whose fault is that?" Martin interrupted.

Mr Wonderful was startled by the bluntness.

"She is a flesh and blood woman with her faults and failures. Flesh and blood, my friend. And you have put her on a pedestal, idolised her. You can't make passionate love to someone you are afraid to break; even I know that."

So simple, so painfully true.

The two men stayed for a while in that cafe, finding solace in each other's honesty for the first time in a long time. A new friendship was forged.

After a few hours had passed, Mr Wonderful made his way back to Eaton Square, to his house. He got changed, read some emails, and made a few calls.

. . .

He was dreading returning to Gabrielle's; he had made a big drama out of nothing, perhaps and wasn't sure how to approach it.

He still had many questions he wanted to ask her. He wanted to know about that Gabrielle she had withheld from him; was it his fault? Was he not satisfying her? But most of all, he needed to know if someone else was in her life now besides him.

Gabrielle was back home; the house was so empty without him. Although the previous evening felt like a step toward getting back to normal, she knew there was still some mending.

She sat at her desk, caressing the old cabinet, hoping her *Mamé* would inspire her on what to do next.

"*Mamé*, what should I do? Speak to me," she said.

Gabrielle had always felt they had a special connection with her grandmother. But, now that she had made her transition, she could feel her energy with her at the most difficult times.

"What can I do now?" she repeated.

And then it came to her: she should write to him.

. . .

Putting words into paper seemed the only way to be fully back in his arms at this point. After all, it was a letter that put a wedge between them. She had always been better at writing than speaking.

She took her notepad and started:
"*My darling, my love.*

I can't be clever or aloof with you: I adore you too much for that.

"Does this sound too 'writersish'?" she wondered. "I don't care. I'm going to write how I feel, no matter how it looks."
… You have no idea how detached I can be with people I don't hold dear.

She paused briefly …

Or perhaps you do. You have shattered my barriers.

"Is he going to think I'm unhappy about it?" she considered.

And I don't begrudge you for it.

She added, just in case.

There are not enough words to tell you what I feel.

. . .

It's a feeling I only get every time you're near, and I fear waking up from this dream.

The whole relationship had felt like a dream from the moment they met until now. A fairy tale, to be precise. She was the damsel in distress, and he was the knight in shining armour who rescued her from herself.

Back in your arms is where I want to be. Once again.

Nothing ever feels so right as when you hold me tight with your arms wrapped around me.

She smiled, thinking about how Mr Wonderful could not fall asleep without holding her and how safe and secure he made her feel.

I nearly forgot what love was like until I met you.

Your first touch, first kiss, the first time you held me close.

"Mr Wonderful is a great kisser." She smiled whilst licking her lips gently. His kisses, a preview of passion simmering beneath the surface. She always wondered about that passion and why it hadn't fully erupted.

. . .

And as time passed, I knew you'd be my last.

I love you more than I ever believed I was capable of.

After the visceral experience with *Le PDG*, she believed she had reached her full capacity for love. But since she had realised he was simply the catalyst to free a part of herself repressed for far too long that was dying to come out. And come out, it did, in a riotous muddled way crumpling all over everything. She hadn't learned how to control these feelings inside of her yet.

Gabrielle paused.

She knew she wasn't addressing the actual 'story': what happened, when and how.

"Do I need to?" Those details were irrelevant to her. She wanted him, most of all, to know about her feelings for him. However, she knew something needed to be said for both of their sake.

You have seen a glimpse into a past long gone and forgotten …
    she wrote …
    A past when I was still searching for myself.

You have shown me so much, more than you'll ever know. You have shown me the best of me, the higher me I had lost.

. . .

Gabrielle loved her reflection in his eyes, being worshipped and adored. He saw her as she aspired to be but was not quite there yet.

It is just impossible for me to say how grateful I am.

"Wait, this sounds bad. Cancel that."

Grateful.

"No, I AM grateful. Very!"

.. truly grateful, she added back.
You make me feel like I can fly.

No matter what she tried, he always encouraged her. Mr Wonderful made her feel empowered and powerful whilst, at the same time, protecting her.

I don't think you comprehend what you do to me because it's impossible to see. I never told you what I feel when you hold my hand.

Gabrielle could feel her stomach churning …

I've found my home in your arms, where I can finally learn to let go. I am still learning.

. . .

"Is it going to be enough?" she pondered.

In your arms, I am at ease; the world disappears, it is only you and I, and nothing else matters.

In your arms, I am free; I can be more than I ever thought possible and be stronger.

You cleaned up the mess and healed my wounds, and now I'm beginning to be whole again.

Gabrielle had felt 'unclean' after Paris.

Even though she always had a very liberal view of sex and relationships, she had always drawn the line to getting involved with men who had any type of commitment. And in Paris, she perpetrated the ultimate sin; an affair with a married man. She remembered how she felt when she had been cheated on.

The anger. The disgust.

Still, it was as if she had an extra-corporeal experience. As if someone else had an affair, not her. She was ashamed. The only thing she had been missing was the more carnal part of herself that she had rediscovered and now had put on hold again. At least until she knew how to control and channel it more positively,

In your arms, I've found my purpose, and there's nothing I can't do, no limits I can't transcend.

In your arms, anything is possible.

In your arms, I find safety like no other, and I can breathe deep, knowing you'll always keep me close and never hurt me.

So please, my darling, hold me close, don't let me go.
    My heart belongs to you. This you must know.
    I want to be here with you, not only for today but forever, in your arms stay.

In your arms, I am home."

Now that she had put her heart to paper, Gabrielle relaxed in the chair.

drip, drop ... , slap, slash, splash ... rat-a-tat-tat

It had started to rain, the drops splattering against the window. She sat there re-reading what she had written and thinking if she should type it but decided against it and copied her words in full into her monogrammed letter sheets.

. . .

Handwritten.

It was getting dark. She folded the letter neatly into an envelope, wrote his name across it, and then left it on the desk.

Mr Wonderful was not back home yet. Gabrielle was debating whether to wait for him or to go out: she had to pop out to pick up some dry cleaning she needed the next day and some groceries. She still hadn't figured out how to approach the subject when she saw him: what to say, how to say, how to hand him the letter.

She looked at her watch. "The dry cleaner will be closing soon; I need to go," she decided.

Mr Wonderful looked at his watch, "It is time to go back to Gabrielle's," he thought.

He called the driver to get the car ready in five minutes while he popped to the florist next door. "Gabrielle loves flowers."

"A dozen pink roses," he said to the florist. An apology bouquet.

The driver dropped him off at the Islington Townhouse. Somehow he felt more at home there than in his own house. Wherever she was, it was home for him.

. . .

"Gabri," he called out as he entered the house.

There was no one there.

He looked around, but she was not in. So he walked up the stairs where the whole kerfuffle started. And there it was; a closed envelope with his name on the bare desk.

He sat down on the same chair where twenty-four hours earlier, he found the other letter. This time though, he opened the envelope with a feeling of anticipation, unfolded the handwritten letter and began to read:

"My darling, my love…
He read slowly, soaking in every word.
… I nearly forgot what love was like until I met you.

He read and re-read it and dissected every word.

You have seen a glimpse into a past long gone and forgotten. A past when I was still searching for myself.

Gabrielle had not really talked about what had happened, but whatever it was, it was now over. In his heart of heart, he believed it.

. . .

As Mr Wonderful looked up, he saw her: Gabrielle was standing in front of him, looking nervous.

It had only been a day, but he had missed holding her and kissing her.

He stood up and walked towards her. Tears were falling down her cheeks.

"I love you," she said.

"I love you too," he replied.

And then she was back in his arms where she belonged.

THE GREATEST LOVE

THE NINE LIVES OF GABRIELLE: FOR THREE, SHE STAYS

"My darling, my love,

I can't be clever or aloof with you: I adore you too much for that.

You have no idea how detached I can be with people I don't hold dear. Or perhaps you do.

You have shattered my barriers. And I don't begrudge you for it.

There are not enough words to tell you what I feel,
It's a feeling I only get every time you're near, and I fear waking from this dream.

Back in your arms is where I want to be once again.
Nothing ever feels so right as when you hold me tight with your arms wrapped around me.

I nearly forgot what love was like until I met you.
Your first touch, first kiss, the first time you held me close.
And as time passed, I knew you'd be my last.
I love you more than I ever believed I was capable of.

You have seen a glimpse into a past long gone and forgotten—a past when I was still searching for myself.

You have shown me so much, more than you'll ever know. You have shown me the best of me, the higher me I had lost.

It is just impossible for me to say how truly grateful I am.

You make me feel like I can fly.

I don't think you comprehend what you do to me because it's impossible to see. I never told you what I feel when you hold my hand.

I've found my home in your arms, where I can finally learn to let go.

In your arms, I am at ease; the world disappears until it is only you and I, and nothing else matters.

In your arms, I am free; I can be more than I ever thought possible and be stronger.

You cleaned up the mess and healed my wounds, and now I'm beginning to be whole again.

In your arms, I've found my purpose, and there's nothing I can't do, no limits I can't transcend.
In your arms, anything is possible.

In your arms, I find safety like no other, and I can breathe deep, knowing you'll always keep me close and never hurt me.

So please, my darling, hold me close, don't let me go.
My heart belongs to you. This you must know.

I want to be here with you, not only for today but forever, in your arms stay.

In your arms, I am home."

D ays had gone by since he had first read it. Mr Wonderful had kept Gabrielle's handwritten note neatly folded in his wallet, the only single reminder of the events. Life had continued unchanged since then.

He was, of course, happy: he could not envision a life without her. But Martin's comments were playing in his head nonstop.

"And whose fault is that?" Martin had said. "She is a flesh and blood woman with her faults and failures. Flesh and blood, my friend."

"Yes, she was," he had discovered in the letter from her ex-lover, "fresh and blood, sweat and tears. He had never seen 'That' Gabrielle," he thought.

"And you have put her on a pedestal, idolised her. You can't make passionate love to someone you are afraid to break; even I know that," Martin had noted.

He was right: Mr Wonderful was afraid to lose and break her; he had idolised her.

"You have shown me the best of me, the higher me I had lost." Gabrielle had written.

. . .

And she was *"truly grateful"* for it, he recalled.

This exalted but fragile version of Gabrielle in his head did not allow him to love her with the unbridled passion he was capable of and to satisfy his needs, nor enable her to be herself. Fully.

"Would he have reacted in the same way to the letter had he not thought of her that way?" the thought mulling in his head repeatedly.

"Probably not," he concluded. His expectations of her and himself were perhaps romantic of a bygone era.

He loved her for what he could see she was underneath her protective shield, and he wanted to protect her.

He loved her for he could be when he was with her.

Deep down in his heart, he knew they both needed to become more 'human.'

Both were enamoured with the idealised version of self when they were together.

"You have shown me the best of me, the higher me I had lost," …drum drum drumming in his head …

. . .

... *"In your arms, I find safety like no other, and I can breathe deep, knowing you'll always keep me close and never hurt me."*

"Safe," he thought, "she feels safe," he repeated.

He knew he always wanted her to feel secure, but not *just* so. He desired to satisfy her deepest needs and wants. ALL of her needs. And his own.

He had lived a very driven, passionate visceral life in every area before, except love, and he wanted that. Needed it. And now he could no longer ignore that; he knew neither could she.

... *"You cleaned up the mess and healed my wounds, and now I'm beginning to be whole again,"* ... *drum drum.*

Something was stopping her, though, and she was not ready to talk about it.

He had noticed that Gabrielle had been particularly caring with him and more demonstrative than usual. He did not know how to encourage her to let go and let him in, if only a little more.

Mr Wonderful folded back the note and put it in his wallet.

. . .

"Time," he said. "It will take time," he repeated to convince himself.

Gabrielle was content that things were back to normal. Mr Wonderful was as chivalrous as usual and had not asked any more questions about the infamous letter.

He looked genuinely surprised and pleased she wrote to him and expressed her feelings.

"It wasn't as painful as I expected," she thought. "I should do it more often," she professed.

But life took over, and she forgot her pledge. Time passed by.

Mr Wonderful, however, wanted to know more, increasingly so. He realised that if he didn't push and prod, she wouldn't volunteer more insights into her past life or soul, for that matter.

"How long was the relationship?" he asked one day.

He knew it had ended but wished to learn more.

"It must have been significant, or she wouldn't have kept that letter."

. . .

"Why has it been so painful?" he couldn't figure it out.

"Why was she holding on and not abandoning herself to sheer pleasure when they were making love?"

One afternoon he had walked in on her as she was pleasuring herself. He stood there and watched silently, unknown to her. He witnessed her sheer abandonment of the flesh and joy in the act. Her face transfixed, her voice raucous.

He watched her touching herself aptly, knowing how to take it slowly or come quickly several times. But not with him. He was beginning to think it WAS him.

Gabrielle always seemed to squirm uncomfortably under his questions, glossing over her answer and changing subjects swiftly.

Mr Wonderful knew he wanted more now. She was capable of more.

He tried to emulate what he had seen her doing.

He touched how she touched herself. He touched her where she touched herself.

. . .

But Gabrielle always managed to hold back to the point that he was sure she was faking orgasm 'to get it over with.'

"He deserved more," he thought.

And it wasn't just about sex, although he felt the need for a more visceral experience. It was about intimacy, the ability and willingness to be vulnerable with each other. And trust.

He had told her about his family, his abusive and philandering father who abandoned his mother and four other brothers, their struggle for a long time and how he made his fortune.

She knew his whole life story. He had been delicate about the details of his past relationships, although most of them had been played out in the press and were common knowledge, at least the gossip. Nevertheless, he had not kept anything from her and had answered any questions she asked.

Sometimes she seemed curious, and he was pleased she was showing an interest. But was not willing or able to do so herself.

Mr Wonderful had lived with Gabrielle in her Islington townhouse and realised she had never even spent the night at his.

He had given her a set of keys and made space in his wardrobe for her. Although he didn't necessarily want to move back or live in Belgravia, he wished she at least tried.

He hoped she did.
    He wanted her to.
    He waited for her to.

Time went by.

Gabrielle returned home from doing some errands to find a set of luggage by the front door. She didn't recognise them.

"Perhaps Mr Wonderful had planned a surprise getaway together?" she thought excitedly.

"Darling?" she called. She looked around and found him upstairs, sitting at her desk with his coat on.

"Hi," she said.

When he looked up, she realised something was wrong.

Mr Wonderful never thought he would ever come to this, saying goodbye.

Gabrielle was staring at him, looking fearful.

· · ·

"My darling," he said. "I think it would be better if we take a break for a while."

Gabrielle looked at him incredulously; she could not believe he was saying that. Tears started falling down her cheeks.

"We can't...."

"Why can't we be together?" she interrupted, weeping.

She was desperate to know why he had to say goodbye. "Surely not; I have misheard him."

She was desperate for him to answer why they couldn't be together.
 They loved each other, didn't they?

"I will always love you," he continued.

He got closer to her and then held her face in his hands while looking into those big brown eyes he fell in love with. He slowly patted her tears dry, trying to be strong for both of them. But it was hard, more difficult than he had imagined, and he couldn't control himself.

He held her a bit longer and told her he would wait for her.

. . .

"My darling, your wounds are still open, and you are the only one who can truly heal them and make yourself whole. Be comfortable with every part of you and what you need and want."

Gabrielle couldn't grasp what he was saying.

"You shouldn't be scared of yourself and what you can be. But my darling, please do know that no matter how long it will take, if you still want me, Io ti aspetto."

She was confused. Soon he told her he would be able to hold her tight and never have to let go again, she heard.

Soon.

But the pain of saying goodbye was too much right now.

"Don't cry," he uttered with tears in his eyes.

'How long am I going to be without you?" she whispered to him. "How long?" she said, sobbing. "Please tell me."

"Don't forget me," he added, unsure how to answer.

"How could I ever?" she thought.

. . .

"I could never live my life fully without you," she said, unable to hold back her emotions, "You are the best part of me," and more tears started pouring down her cheeks.

"Let's make a date," he then declared. He was too scared, leaving it open-ended. He needed a date to look forward to.

"Let's meet on top of the Empire State Building," he proposed, hopeful. They had watched *An Affair to Remember* many times together, and both loved how sweepingly romantic it was.

Gabrielle smiled through her tears, nodding.

"Six months from today," he was aching, thinking how he could live without her for so long. He knew though she needed the time.

"I will wait for you," he brought her closer to him as he wrapped his arms around her, time slipping out of his grip.

"I love you."

Mr Wonderful hugged her tighter. Hoping that if he held on tighter to her, he wouldn't have to leave her.

. . .

Then he kissed her gently on the forehead, and, just like that, he was gone—every sign of him. The driver had picked up his luggage.

Gabrielle sat in silence for hours. Deep, profound emptiness inside of her.

The next day she received a plane ticket to New York dated precisely six months.

"Io ti aspetto," the accompanying note said.

Tears started streaming down her face when she thought she had no more to spare. In the following weeks, Paola and Martin rallied around her and tried their best to keep her company.

But, slowly, she found herself alone, starting again.

A long time passed before she could fully comprehend why he was gone.

"I love you," …. she murmured into the hot embrace they were sharing, but soon she felt her hands hold on to nothingness.

She woke up and opened her eyes slowly, scared to come to a reality where he was gone.

. . .

But once she did, Gabrielle realised she was alone once again. She wrapped her arms around herself. Holding herself, trying to feel his warmth again.

"I love you!" She shouted into the empty space, hoping wherever he was, he heard her.

Days and months went by.

Gabrielle's nightmares gradually subsided, replaced by vivid, joyful memories. Slowly but surely, she had begun to find her way back to herself. And she owed that to him.

She could see now.

Gabrielle had found her inner Isadora Duncan once again and learned to channel her desire and lust for life positively for her greater good. Not just in her new creative career this time.

Instead of comparing now to the future or the past, she lived entirely in the present, savouring every moment.

With the death of her old self that she'd long been expecting and the birth of another, happier, higher one, Gabrielle stood erect and strong, drawing high and higher, until her stretched-out wings broke into fire.

. . .

She finally found a place to stand still, in love.

Your task is not to seek for LOVE,
but merely to seek and find all the barriers within yourself
that you have built against it

Rumi

PART IV

THE NINE LIVES OF GABRIELLE: FOR THREE, SHE …

Sometimes nine lives are not enough …

IO TI ASPETTO

THE NINE LIVES OF GABRIELLE: FOR THREE, SHE …

M r Wonderful struggled to keep his composure; Gabrielle was looking at him incredulously, a mix of pain and disbelief showing on her beautiful face. It took all his strength to disentangle himself from Gabrielle and their last embrace.

As he walked out, he could hear her sobbing and murmuring, "Don't leave me, please don't leave me." He knew that he couldn't turn or he would never leave.

George, his driver, had taken his luggage into the Rolls and was waiting outside. The car door was open, and he slid in as quickly as possible.

"Home, sir?" George asked. "Yes, Eaton Square," he replied.

It had been a long time since he called it home. George kept looking at Mr Wonderful through the rearview mirror. The Boss looked distraught; he had never seen him like that before, and he never lost his cool or showed anger or pain. But, on the other hand, George had never seen him so happy as when he met and moved in with Gabrielle.

He could sense this was a delicate moment. George had been with Mr Wonderful since his twenties and had seen him grow his empire. He had never changed, always worked hard, and was always respectful of all people, no matter the circumstances and where they came from. And as his fortune and status grew, so did his generosity and kindness toward people.

. . .

Yes, he had high standards, but that is to be expected. Mr Wonderful was the son he never had. As they arrived at the empty house, Mr Wonderful made a bee-line for his office and closed the door behind him.

"What's up with him?" asked the maid.

"It's Sir to you," George added quickly, annoyed.

She left quickly, scolded. George went into the kitchen and asked Maria, his wife, housekeeper and factotum, "Can you prepare your famous stew, darling?"

"What's wrong?" Maria immediately asked. She used to make it when Mr Wonderful was down or missing his mother. It was her recipe and his favourite comforting dish.

"He is back home," George responded.

"Oh, ah," she sighed, upset. Maria cared deeply about Mr Wonderful and could see his love for Gabrielle. She hoped in her heart they would get married one day.

"I'll start on it straight way," she said.

Mr Wonderful sat at his desk for hours, replaying every second of his last meeting with Gabrielle. He remembered every single expression on her face. It was the most difficult and painful decision of his life. He had to muster all his strength and courage to carry it through.

And now, now he was regretting it already.

"She needs the time to grow and understand who she really is and what she wants—not being scared of herself and being able to love with her full intensity without holding back," he said to reassure himself.

But already he missed her. Mr Wonderful wanted to be with her, smell her perfume, caress every inch of her face and body, kiss her, be inside her. Gabrielle was everything he always wanted. His heart and body were aching for her already.

Heart and mind.

The heart knew, always knew.

On the other hand, the mind wanted to be sure if Gabrielle was with him because she felt safe, because she loved how he loved her, respectfully, or if she really loved him.

It was getting dark.

Knock knock.

. . .

"Yes?" the door opened slowly, and Maria entered the room. The smell wafting from the serving tray in her hands told him she had cooked his mother's stew, Solyanka, his favourite.

"Bless her," he thought, "she is looking after me."

"Thank you," he said out loud.

He was not hungry but appreciated the gesture. George and Maria have been with him for over twenty-five years and were like family. They came with him when he moved from New York to London; he could trust them implicitly.

Maria closed the door behind her. The smell of the food was slowly breaking down his resistance. He started to eat slowly. The photograph of his mother was on his desk, looking at him warmly. He could feel his mother's love with every sip and slurp.

"мама, what did I do?"

Gabrielle was standing by the window, her bowl of hot steamy coffee in her hands, looking down at Canonbury Gardens. Children were playing while the mothers were chit-chatting with one another.

. . .

Six months had gone by so quickly. Gabrielle was happy and serene and had reached a level of self-acceptance and self-love like never before. And she owed it all to him, Mr Wonderful.

She would have never dug that deep if he hadn't shocked her into it. The day he left and the weeks and months after, she pined for him, longing to feel safe ad loved, longing for his touch.

Pining and longing turning into anger and resentment. "How dare he? He said he loved me and would always be there for me."

Slowly but surely, though, Gabrielle came to understand what he did and why. Gabrielle had 'half-loved' him, 'half-given' herself to him. She had been holding herself back from him, from love and most importantly, from life. He had made the ultimate sacrifice; let her go so she could find herself and grow.

"Still, why didn't he ever contact me?" she sometimes wondered, perplexed. She was tempted at the beginning to beg him to come back. But she never did.

Pride.

Now Gabrielle was happy she didn't. She was pleased with herself and her life.

· · ·

Finally.

Fully.

Now the only thing that was missing was him. Not as a crutch, protection. Not because she loved how she looked reflected in his eyes but because she missed him.

Desperately.

"Did he still love her? Did he still want her? Will he be there waiting?"

She had seen pictures of him with famous people. The paps snapped him outside the swanky London restaurant The Twenty-Two. He appeared to be in a good mood, smiling, wearing a black shirt, dark blue jeans, and black boots on the evening outing, with his brown locks parted to the side and his custom-made platinum watch. A pang of jealousy squeezed her heart.

And now, the time had come.

"Dear Ms Arkin, we look forward to welcoming you to our hotel."

. . .

"He would tell me if he had changed his mind; he wouldn't let me go all the way to New York and not show up," she thought while reading the email from The Langham. Mr Wonderful had booked and paid for a suite for a long weekend.

"Meeting at the top of the Empire State Building after six months, just like *An Affair to Remember*, was so painstakingly romantic," she thought.

"I better get ready now, " she said, looking at her watch.

Gabrielle was meeting Paola for lunch at the 2 Veneti, an Italian restaurant close to Oxford Circus tube station.

She arrived early and decided to wait inside, pleased with herself and how far she had come in the last six months. In the past, they would have met by the nearest tube station, or Gabrielle would have waited outside the restaurant for Paola to arrive instead of going in alone.

Not now.

She calmly and confidently went in and ordered their favourite sparkling wine while waiting, a bottle of Prosecco di Treviso.

The 2 Veneti is a friendly and understated restaurant; both women loved the food's bold, authentic flavours and specialities, mainly from Veneto, and enjoyed the very understated, friendly, and elegant manner.

"Ciao Ciccia," Paola said as she approached the table. "Ciao Bella," and the two women embraced.

"Ti trovo bene, you look great," she added.

"I feel great," Gabrielle responded.

"Are you ready to order?" the waiter asked.

"Un Carpaccio di Manzo for starter and un Fritto Misto Veneziano for main," Gabrielle answered while Paola was reading the menu.

"I'll have the Carpaccio too," said Paola sipping her prosecco, "and un Filetto di Cernia."

The restaurant was a total capacity and slightly noisy, adding to the Italian ambience and culture where eating is all about simple food and animated conversation at the dinner table. Nevertheless, the service was attentive and friendly, as always.

"Allora Ciccia, the time has come. How are you feeling? Are you going to take the plunge and go?" Paola jumped in, curious.

. . .

"Si," Gabrielle nodded, apprehensive of Paola's reaction.

"Have you called him? Texted? To say if everything is still on? You know, six months is a long time," Paola went on unperturbed.

"No, I haven't. He would tell me, I'm sure."

"How long are you staying?" Paola asked.

"I don't know. Hopefully, for a while," Gabrielle answered, hopeful.

"I'm going to Italy tomorrow to visit mamma."

Gabrielle looked at her.

"Yes, a rumpy-pumpy with Marco too," Paola said.

"Is it still going on?"

"Needs are needs."

For once, now, Gabrielle understood perfectly.

• • •

They took their time over lunch; the conversation was flowing. Finally, the time came to go.

"Text me when you arrive in New York. And if you need, call me," Paola said.

"I will, thank you," and after a long hug, they parted company.

Mr Wonderful was meeting Martin for a pint in Central London. The two men had formed a solid friendship since the infamous dinner. Better still, since the heartfelt chat they had the morning after.

The met regularly for a drink after work. Martin could talk openly about Paola's affair, his insecurities and fears and Mr Wonderful could talk about Gabrielle and ask Martin for updates.

He had purposely not contacted her to give her space but was dying to know if she was OK. So besides watching her on YouTube and buying her latest book, he was keeping an eye from a safe distance.

"Two pints of lager, please," Martin ordered with the bartender.

"So, how are you doing?"

"I'm OK," Martin replied, "Paola is going to Italy tomorrow; the girls are staying with my mother."

．　．　．

Mr Wonderful knew what he meant: Paola was meeting with her lover.

"Have you contacted Gabrielle? Time is getting closer."

"No, I haven't. I don't want her to feel pressurised. It has to be her decision."

"Man, this is crazy. You surely can't go to New York and wait at the top of the Empire State Building without knowing if she will show up. I know New York is home for you, but still, it's crazy," Martin said.

"Have you told Paola you know about her and her Italian stud?"

Martin's cheeks went red. "Touché," he replied.

"Gabrielle has everything she needs if she wants to come over and see me: plane ticket, hotel reservation. She just needs to be sure she still wants it. She still wants me, us."

"What did you book a hotel room for? Why can't she stay with you?"

．　．　．

"You know, in case she wants to take things slow. It has been six months, after all."

"Do you hear yourself?" Martin went on, "You are still treating her like a delicate flower. If she is coming to New York is because she wants to be back with you. Why come otherwise? You are a hopeless old-fashioned romantic."

Mr Wonderful looked at Martin, nodding. He couldn't help himself when it came to Gabrielle.

"I still think you should contact her to see if she is coming," Martin added.

"I still think you should tell Paola you know," Mr Wonderfull continued.

"What a pair we are," the two men nodded in agreement.

"I'm leaving tomorrow; I have some family business to attend to, and I want to get everything ready," Mr Wonderful declared.

"Where are you flying from?" Martin asked to make conversation.

"Stansted," he replied.

. . .

"Stansted? I didn't know they had direct flights to New York from there ..." Martin asked, surprised.

"They don't. I have my plane," Mr Wonderful clarified.

"Uuuh, fancy," Martin said with a smirk. He had always known he was a big shot. He hadn't realised perhaps how big. He was always so understated, a nice guy.

"Yes, very" Mr Wonderful flashed one of his dazzling smiles.

"Gosh, you are so f***ing handsome. If I weren't straight and already married, I would fancy you for myself," Martin declared.

Mr Wonderful laughed.

"Let me know if you learn something after I've gone, will you?" he said.

"Will do," Martin said.

Mr Wonderful made his way to Stansted early the next day. He needed to be in New York to sort out some of his late father's property.

. . .

He hadn't quite realised what malarky it was to inherit such a vast estate and title. He needed some days to meet various organisations under his patronage.

He wanted enough time to sort everything out and get ready for Gabrielle.

To make their meeting special and magical.

He spent the flight reading papers and replying to emails. The plane finally touched down. A car was waiting for him. As he disembarked the aircraft, he turned toward the ocean.

"Baby, are you coming? Io sono qui. Io ti aspetto."

" I will wait for you as long as it takes.
I will love you every moment
Across time"
- Lauren Kate

RUN TO YOU

THE NINE LIVES OF GABRIELLE: FOR
THREE, SHE …

"Passport, boarding pass, reservation, all here," Gabrielle said to herself, checking her handbag to ensure she had everything.

She was nervous. The Uber was waiting outside. As she turned the key, she felt like exhaling. New York was going to be another adventure, the biggest of them all.

"Baby, I'm coming," looking out the car window.

Now she couldn't wait; she just wanted to run to him, back in his arms, once and for all.

The trip to Heathrow seemed so long this time. She was on the 8.25 am flight, landing in New York JFK mid-morning, giving her plenty of time to freshen up and get ready to meet him early evening.

Gabrielle checked in her luggage and went through departures, waiting impatiently for the screens to signal it was time for boarding.

Paola had been texting her to ensure she was OK and wish her good luck.

She realised her phone batteries were running low and had inadvertently packed the charger.

. . .

"Never mind," she thought.

The wait seemed endless. Finally, the screen started showing the gate; her heart was pounding.

It was finally happening. She was going to see him again. Soon. She smiled as she walked towards the gate. The flight attendants rechecked the boarding passes and passports. And then more waiting. And waiting, and waiting.

"We should have boarded the plane by now," she thought.

She could see the other passengers getting restless, going towards the desk, and asking questions. She didn't want to make a nuisance of herself, but after a while, she began to worry.

"Hi," she greeted the lady behind the desk, "What is happening? Why haven't we boarded yet?"

"We are waiting for instruction, Madam," she replied.

And they waited, and waited, and waited some more.

Then, eventually, Gabrielle texted Paola to inform her of the delay.

. . .

"Still plenty of time to check in at the hotel and get ready," she thought.

Time was passing by. Finally, they started boarding.

All passengers were on the plane now. More time went by. The flight attendants conspicuously absent.

More time.

"Ladies and gentlemen. Welcome aboard British Airways BA0117 flight to New York JFK. We are currently held on the platform as we missed our turn. Sorry for the inconvenience," the captain said over the intercom.

And so they waited for some more. The flight was now over three hours late, and Gabrielle worried. Her phone was on its last breath.

"Should she call him? Text him? Something."

As much as it would be far more romantic to meet him on the top of the Empire State building, she didn't want him to think she was not coming. So she started frantically writing a text when the batteries died, just like that.

. . .

"Ladies and gentlemen, we have received confirmation we can depart. Crew prepare for take off. Again, please accept our apologies for the delay," the captain announced.

The flight attendants were now getting the passengers and plane ready to take off. It was time to go.

Time is a funny thing. Sometimes it seems to fly. Sometimes it seems to stand still. Today was the latter, one of those days. The flight seemed to take ages. Longer than usual. The plane delay meant it would be a rush all the way through.

"I can still make it in time," she hoped, crossing her fingers.

The plane finally landed at JFK at 14.55 and then held on the runaway for another forty-five minutes, waiting for a parking spot.

The long wait was finally over. They started to off-board and walk toward immigration. Gabrielle still remembered her first time in New York and her not-so-glorious experience with a Border Patrol bossy Officer.

"Ma'am, stand behind the yellow line," the voice still ringing in her ears.

Fortunately, the experience was much more pleasant this time.

However, there were more checks due to the Coronavirus and related precautions.

Gabrielle waited patiently for her luggage to come around the carousel. She needed more than hand luggage for this trip; she'd hoped to stay much longer than a weekend.

Perhaps he would show her around where he grew up, New York through his eyes. Maybe she would meet his family. She knew how close they were.

"Excuse me, M'am is that your luggage," a stranger asked her. "She jolted back into reality and realised her luggage was the only one going around and around the carousel.

She had been daydreaming. "Yes, thank you," she responded.

"Shit, shit, shit," she thought, grabbing her case and rushing to the taxi rank.

"The Langham Hotel, Fifth Avenue, please," she said to the driver.

Of course, all things come in three. So the traffic had to be particularly bad.

"An accident," the taxi driver explained.

. . .

Gabrielle looked at her watch.

She started feeling a grip in her stomach, and her eyes were tearing up. After all this, after the past six months, she was going to be late.

"What if he doesn't wait?"

"Chelsea, please can you check with British Airways if Ms Arkin has boarded the plane from London to JFK?" Mr Wonderful asked one of the secretaries.

"Sir, I don't think …" he had put down the phone. "I don't think they'd tell you these things anymore," she continued, talking to herself, shaking her head.

She checked with the airline anyway, but, of course, they wouldn't confirm. The only thing they did confirm was that the flight was late.

"Sir," she buzzed him back, "the plane left Heathrow late. The airline cannot confirm if Ms Arkin had boarded." Mr Wonderful sounded annoyed and preoccupied, "But it was my credit card."

"Yes, Sir, unfortunately, it does not matter who paid for the flight. They still would not confirm. Security reasons."

· · ·

His PA got the gist of the conversation and noticed the tension in the air, "I'll take over from here."

"Sir, I'll check with the hotel to see if they've received a confirmation of stay and ask them to inform us when she has checked in," she added.

"Thank you," he responded.

Time was going slowly today. He checked his phone to see if Gabrielle had sent a text or email.

No.

Nothing.

Knock knock.

"Sir, The Langham has not received a confirmation. However, they were not expecting one," she explained, noticing his expression.

"They are aware, though, that the plane is considerably late," she added.

· · ·

"Thank You."

Doubts started creeping in again.

"Gabri, baby, are you coming? Do you still love me?" he muttered. "Perhaps I should have listened to Martin and found out before today," he thought.

The meeting was at 18.30, and he had set up a special surprise for them at the top. Everything was in order as planned.

He started getting ready hours ahead. He was incredibly nervous. He showered, put some aftershave on and wore something smart but not too formal or casual.

He chose something he knew Gabrielle liked. His office in Manhattan was a short distance from the Empire State Building. Nevertheless, he started making his way early. He wanted to check everything in person.

Everybody greeted him profusely; a special concierge had been assigned to look after his every need. Everyone knew who he was.

"Mr Fitzwilliam, everything is ready for you," the concierge said as they went through every minute detail.

. . .

Time was getting closer and closer.

Ring ring.

"Yes?"

"Sir. The plane shows as landing four hours late," his PA said on the phone. "There is a road accident blocking the road to Manhattan," she added.

"Thanks for letting me know," Mr Wonderful replied.

"Gabry baby, are you on your way? Were you on that plane?" he thought, anxious.

More time went by.

17.30.

Mr Wonderful was there, waiting for her, longing to see her again.

"Any time now," he thought.

17.50.

. . .

18.00.

Ring ring.

"Yes?"

"Tom?" his younger brother on the phone. "Tom, there was an accident. Michael is at NYU," he added.

Silence.

"Tom, Tom, are you there?"

Mr Wonderful was stunned.

"Yes, I am here. How bad is Micky?" he asked.

"He is unconscious at the moment; we are all here."

"I'm coming," Mr Wonderful said.

He called George to explain the situation.
     "Please, can you come over to the Empire State and wait for

Gabrielle? Tell her what happened. If she arrives, can you take her to NYU?"

"When she arrives, you mean" George corrected him reassuringly.

"Yes, when she arrives."

"I'll take her there; I make my way now," he added.

Mr Wonderful rushed to the hospital. He always looked after his mother and brothers; he was the protector and provider of the family after their father left.

Gabrielle arrived at the hotel at 18.45. Too late to check in and freshen up. Most importantly late for the meeting with Mr Wonderful.

The porter opened the taxi door and greeted her warmly; she smiled faintly, too preoccupied with rushing towards the concierge.

"Gabrielle Arkin," she said. "I'm late for an appointment. Is it OK if I leave my luggage here somewhere for now?"

"Good evening Ma'am, we were expecting you, no problem at all," replied the concierge.

. . .

"How do I get to …?" Gabrielle started.

"The Empire State Building is just three minute's walk from here; Manuel will accompany you," he added quickly.

They were expecting her, indeed.

"Thank you so much," grateful.

As they arrived at the building, there was a long queue. She could feel the panic rising.

"This way, Ma'am," Manuel guided her through the crowd and towards a gentleman in a burgundy uniform. He seemed to recognise Manuel and walked over to greet her.

"Good evening and welcome to The Empire State Building; how can I help you?"

"I am here to meet Mr Vitale?" she said. " We are supposed to meet at the top?" she clarified.

The man looked perplexed. "Vitale, you said?" to confirm.

. . .

"Yes," Gabrielle answered, "Tom Vitale. I am Gabrielle Arkin."

The man's face showed signs of recognition after hearing her name.

"Ah yes, I don't have a Mr Vitale, sorry," he said. "Mr Fitzwilliam was expecting you. Unfortunately, he is gone."

"Fitzwilliam?" she thought.

"Gone?" she repeated to confirm.

"Yes, he left not long ago, Ma'am," he replied.

Gabrielle nodded. Tears started streaming down her cheeks.

He's gone. He must have thought I wasn't coming. Not for a minute, it had crossed her mind he wouldn't be there. He didn't wait.

"Ma'am, are you OK?"

"Yes, thank you."

• • •

Gabrielle started walking out of the building. The happy faces of the tourist waiting in the queue staring.

"Ma'am, can I accompany you back to the hotel?" Manuel asked.

"No, thank you. I'll be alright," she replied.

She stood still under the blurred New York lights, watching people go by. Stunned.

"Baby, I came. I came for you."

" In your arms;
that's where I always want to be"
- Idlehearts.com

IT WAS ALWAYS YOU

THE NINE LIVES OF GABRIELLE: FOR
THREE, SHE …

"**M**s Arkin? Ms ..." Gabrielle she heard as she was walking back toward the hotel. She turned around and saw George rushing toward her, out of breath, waving.

"Ms Arkin?" he said again.

She had never been happier to see someone.
    "George, so happy to see you," smiling through her tears.

He could see how distraught she was and updated her on the events as quickly as possible.

"I am here to take you to the hospital; if you want to go, that is?" he asked.

"Yes, yes," Gabrielle nodded.

"My car is there," he pointed.

George was looking at Gabrielle through the rearview mirror. She looked worried and tearing up, but at least she was here. He had his doubts but never shared them with Mr Wonderful.

"Is it far?" she asked.
    "No, only 3 kilometres. There is just some evening traffic to go through."
    She nodded.

. . .

As they entered the building, Gabrielle looked lost. Thank God George was there and knew where to go.

"This way," he said. Then, as they were walking, George saw Mr Wonderful in the seating area, his head in his hands, surrounded by his brothers. The wait had been agonising.

Waiting for Gabrielle.
    Waiting for the doctors to tell them something. Anything.

"Sir?"

He looked up and saw George, alone. His eyes searched. And then, just behind him, Gabrielle.

His hands were wet and sticky; he was so nervous. She was there. She was actually there. He started walking towards her when she sprinted into his arms. The long passionate embrace, their cheeks touching, his breath on her neck, her breath in his ear. He was so aroused that he dared not release her from his embrace. He was so hard that he'd feared it'd show.

"I guess you are happy to see me," she smiled.

"Cheeky," he smiled too. "Obviously."

. . .

His sparkling blue eyes were full of unreleased tears.

"You came; you are here. Sorry, I had to leave", he said.

"I was late; I am sorry I was late," Gabrielle apologised.

"it was not your fault, baby," holding her face in his hands. "You are here. That is all that matters," he added.

"I'm so sorry about your brother," she asked.
    "Yes, thank you."
    "Do you know ..?"
    "Not yet; we are waiting."

Mr Wonderful waved at George.
    "Thank you" moving his lips.

His brothers were starting to gather around them when the surgeon came out of the swinging doors.

The doctor went straight toward Mr Wonderful.

"He is still in critical condition, Viscount. He has suffered a brain injury. We had to medically induce a coma to prevent intracranial hypertension and allow the brain to recuperate."

. . .

They all stood there, stunned.

"There is nothing you can do here. He is in intensive care. We will call you if anything happens," the doctor added.

"We are not leaving," voices rising.

"Thank you, Doctor," Mr Wonderful took charge.

"There is no reason for all of us to stay. We can take turns," he said.

"We can stay," Gabrielle intervene, holding Mr Wonderful's arm. She knew he wanted to stay but wouldn't say because of her.

He turned to look at her. "We can do the first shift," she continued.

"Yes," taking it from where she left off, "You all have families waiting for you, go."

"I'll call if anything happens," he continued.

"I'll do the night. I'll come back later after the children are in bed," his brother Paul said.

. . .

After some more talks and hugs, the others left.

"Sir, shall I wait for you?" George was still there.

"There's no need, George, thank you. We will take a cab," Mr Wonderful responded.

"They were finally alone. Alone in a hospital waiting room. Not exactly what he had planned," he was thinking, feeling guilty.

"You hungry?" he asked her.

"Not really, but I could do with a coffee," Gabrielle replied.

"It's machine coffee," knowing how particular she was about coffee.

"It's fine." She had yet to let go of his arm.

They walked together to the dispensing machine and settled down in the corner of the waiting area.

Mr Wonderful was thinking how much he wanted her right there and then and feeling totally inappropriate for it.

. . .

She was sitting beside him, looking at him, holding the plastic coffee cup with both her hands. A quizzing look in her eyes.

"When I arrived at the Empire State, I asked for you, and the man didn't seem to know you," she blurted out, unable to hold her curiosity any longer.

He had a puzzled look, and his eyebrows crumpled.

"I asked for Mr Vitale. He called you Fitzwilliam. You are not some double agent spy, are you?" she added, trying to make a joke of it. "Had he been hiding something from her?" she was, however, thinking.

"You are watching and reading far too much detective drama," he smiled.

"You are both right," he added. Gabrielle looked even more perplexed. His hand was on her thigh, caressing her; she couldn't think straight.

"Long story," Mr Wonderful went on.

Gabrielle was getting warmer by the minute, the gentle stroke arousing her like crazy.

. . .

"We have time," she smiled, "I always assumed you were kind of Italian origins. Fitzwilliam is not very Italian."

"Italian?" a quizzical look on his face, " Ah!" recognising what she meant, "No. It was Vitalik. My maternal grandparents changed it when they arrived in the United States from Russia. They settled around Brooklyn, so Vitale seemed appropriate."

"She smelled so good," he was thinking, imagining what she was wearing underneath her cashmere jumper.

"My parents were never married," he continued, trying to keep together.

"My father was some aristocrat from Ireland who wanted to be bohemian and independent from his family obligations. So, he moved to the U.S. to escape his family and do 'his thing'. He met my mother, and things progressed from there" he looked bitter.

"One kid after another, they soon found themselves with five children. I am the eldest."

Gabrielle's eyes were open wide. He had told her before about the father leaving.

"One set of twins," he continued.

.   .   .

"Well, between his gambling and womanising and all the responsibilities, life was too hard for him," Mr Wonderful said sarcastically.

"One day, he just left, took all his things, and we never saw again. He returned to his father with his tail between his legs, begged for forgiveness (and money), and married some other aristocrat."

Gabrielle put the cup of coffee on the small table in the waiting area and wrapped herself around his arm.

"He must have worked out more than usual. His muscles were even stronger and more compact," she thought. "STOP IT, Gabri."

"They couldn't have children. Then his wife died, and he started getting sick eight years ago. He came clean and told his father he had children after all—he had an heir to the family name," he went on.

"Wow," Gabrielle blurted out.

"Yes, can you believe it? He never told them? My grandparents never knew about us until then. My father used an alias in the U.S.."

"Sounds like a movie," Gabrielle said.

. . .

He continued to caress her longer, deeper strokes inside the thigh, up .... and down...

"My father passed away shortly after his revelation. I got to know my grandfather for a while before he also passed away three years ago. My paternal grandmother is still with us."

"Viscount?" she recalled the doctor calling him.

"When my grandfather died, the title passed on to me, the firstborn," Mr Wonderful continued, "I am still getting used to it."

"Go on, tell me," Gabrielle was curious.

"Viscount Thomas Darcy Vitale Fitzwilliam III," he said.

"Don't ..." his finger on the tip of her nose, " don't laugh ... "

"Darcy Fitzwilliam?" Gabrielle was amused.

"Not funny. My mother was a big Austen fan. I'm grateful to him for at least one thing: he stopped her from naming me Darcy."

. . .

"Guess?" she then asked. Mr Wonderful looked puzzled.

"Guess my middle name," she went on.

"Not Elizabeth, is it?" with a quizzical look.

"Indeed it is. Nothing to do with Austen. I am named after my two grandmothers: Gabrielle and Elizabeth."

"If we had known, we could have just skipped to the end of the story," she said, resting her head on his chest, his arm around her.

"Hello, love birds" Paul startled them; he was back.

"How is Mickey?" he inquired.

"Still no news," Mr Wonderful responded.

"It is time for the two of you to go," Paul proceeded. "Go, go; I'll call if there is any news," he added to reassure them.

"We will be close by."

"Ok."

· · ·

"See you in the morning."

They walked out of the hospital gloating, their feet almost not touching the ground; they were hungry for each, literally starving.

Mr Wonderful grabbed a taxi as it was passing by.
   "The Langham, Fifth Avenue," he said.

Of course, such a short ride did not amuse the taxi driver, but the $ 50 tip seemed to appease him—a lot.

They arrived at the hotel shortly after. Gabrielle remembered she still needed to check-in.

"You'll be fine," he said.

"Viscount, so pleased to see you," Mr Wonderful nodded, "Ms Arkin, your luggage is in your room," the concierge said as he handed her the key.
   "Welcome, and have a pleasant stay."

They both rushed to the lift, dying to be alone.

· · ·

She couldn't open and close the bedroom door behind them fast enough.

He started kissing her face and her neck, caressing her breast.

Gabrielle yanked his jacket off his shoulder and onto the floor.

His hands down to her waist, unzipping her jeans.

She undid his belt and the zip and pulled his trousers and boxers down his tights.

Their trousers down their ankles, they started moving, hopping towards the bed, kissing, panting.

"Shit," they tumbled on the floor. It always seemed so easy in the movies, where everything happens so smoothly, not so much in real life.

Gabrielle was on top of Mr Wonderful. "Ouch," she moaned.

"You OK?" he asked as he kicked his trousers off him.

"Yes," she replied. He got up, stark naked from his waist down, pulled her onto his shoulder, and then threw her on the bed.

Their lovemaking was unbridled, unrestricted, and wild. And quick. The long wait at the hospital a prolonged and agonising foreplay.

. . .

They lay there exhausted, still half-dressed, the bed covers all over the floor, neither saying anything. For the first time, there was nothing to add. They were with each other exactly where they were meant to be.

"I need to shower, " Gabrielle said after a while.

"Can I join you?" he asked with a cheeky smile.

"I was hoping you would," she added. They jumped into a hot, long shower, Mr Wonderful working his magic with the shower head.

"Oh Tom, God Tom," she shouted.

"Not God, just Tom. But if you insist, though, Viscount will do," he said, flashing a smile.

She was too involved even to laugh.

"I have been perfecting my shower skill, you like?" he added.

"Love them!" Gabrielle screamed.

Their lovemaking lasted off and on all night, not a wink of sleep, both sustained by adrenaline.

. . .

The sun was rising in New York.

"Do you want to get some sleep while I go back to the hospital? I must be exhausted," Mr Wonderful asked thoughtfully.

"I'll come with you; plenty of time to sleep," Gabrielle answered, not wanting to be apart from him, not even for a minute, especially now that she could be there for him like he always had for her.

The next few days went by, long days and nights at the hospital and family get-togethers. Then, one day, Michael recovered and was moved out of intensive care into a private room. After that, life started to get back to normal.

Gabrielle had fit in smoothly with the family and got to know Mr Wonderful's grandmother via FaceTime. But, unfortunately, she was too fragile to travel from Ireland.

"Where did you hide this lovely girl Thomas?" she asked.
    "You both must come over as soon as Michael is better for 'you know what', wink wink", she said one day with a twinkle in her eye.

"What was that?" Gabrielle asked once the call was over.

. . .

"What?" he replied, pretending nothing had happened.

"You know, she said 'for you know what'. You know what, what?"

Mr Wonderful looked deeply into her eyes and took a small Tiffany box out of his pocket. He had been carrying it around since she arrived. He had planned a grand proposal at the top of the Empire State Building; a quartet of violinists, champagne, and red roses, but then the call, Michael, everything. Since then, he had been waiting for the right time.

He opened the box and went down on one knee.

"Baby, will you marry me?"

The ring was an exquisite 18K Tiffany Schlumberger engagement ring with diamonds and emeralds, which he had searched and searched for since they met. Gabrielle recognised the vintage piece from the Faerber collection; she started crying uncontrollably.

"Yes, yes," nodding.

"It was always you. It was always you."

" Love isn't perfect;
It isn't a fairytale or a storybook and
it doesn't always come easy.
Love is overcoming obstacles, facing challenges,
fighting to be together , holding on and never letting go.
It is a short word, easy to spell, difficult to define,
and impossible to live without.
Love is work, but most of all,
love is realising that every hour, every minute,
every second of it was worth it
because you did it together"

- UNKNOWN

AFTERWORD

Intensity-seeking is an enslavement of our perpetuation.

Our healing journey can begin when we step out of the madness of always pursuing someone new and instead meet the same old unhappy, and lonely self. Draining ourselves with newness is a defence against ourselves, which we cannot outrun.

Vulnerability is where courage and fear meet. It is awkward and scary, but it is also freedom and liberation.

Being uniquely you: embracing your imperfections and daring to be vulnerable, engaging fully and openly with the world around you, being open despite knowing it might hurt you, and feeling love, belonging and joy. It feels like going out without makeup, with no armour hoping the real you isn't too disappointing. And still feeling worthy.

Ouch! I know it sounds scary.

Once you stop searching externally, you can finally be the

authentic, joyous person you were born to be and find a love that is deserving of you.

Realise that you ARE worthy. Right here, right now. Perfectly imperfect and absolutely fabulous.

Laura xxx

HER LITTLE SECRET

" Your past does not define you
unless you live there"
- Tony Robbins

GUESS WHAT?

PAOLA

The sun is struggling to break through the thick clouds, casting a faint ray of light across the back garden. The aroma of freshly brewed coffee permeates the kitchen: strong, rich, and familiar. I inhale deeply and savour the moment. I step out onto the patio, and the cool mist dampens my skin. The surrounding trees are shrouded in ghostly white. I wrap my dressing gown tight and sit to gather my thoughts. Martin is still asleep. I love these moments alone before the hustle and bustle of the day begins, lost in my thoughts.

"Come back to bed; I want to be inside you one more time," Marco's ruffled salt and pepper hair caresses his face, tight muscle visible under his tanned skin.

"No, I need to go; I have to get ready, and I have a plane to catch." I rush toward the bathroom and lock the door behind me, "Please, don't follow me," I hope silently. Marco is so masculine; he makes me weak at the knees. The bastard is so arrogant, so secure of himself, I could slap him sometimes. He annoys me so much, his controlling ways. Yet I am so turned on and can't stay away—time after time.

Bang bang!

"Common Paola, common, let me in," he says through the closed door. "You know how much you like my shower trick."

Bang bang!

"Paola, stop being a bitch; I want to fuck you one more time before you go. Open the door; it is an order."

I tremble at the thought of his fingers inside me, and I hate myself for it.

Click.

"That's a good girl. This is what you came for, after all, a good fuck." Marco is standing there, proud of his nakedness, fully erect. He rips my gown open, grabbing my breasts.

"Ouch," the nipples still sore from last night.

"On your knees. Now!"

· · ·

"I am in a rush … I can't …"

"I don't care, on your knees."

Swish—the noise in the kitchen jolts me out of my reveries. I am wet. Damn. Each trip back is heavier and heavier.

Sip, sip.

How did I get into this? Each time, he wants more, more than I can give, and I feel dirtier every time. Yet...

The iPad on the kitchen table buzzes a FaceTime call. Gabrielle from New York. A slender hand with the most humongous diamond and emerald on the ring finger greets me.

"Ciccia, you are going to need some scaffolding on your wrist to carry that. Wow!"

Gabrielle is beaming as she admires the ring. "It's a vintage Tiffany Schlumberger from the Faerber collection. Tom had searched and searched for it since we'd met. He remembered!" a tear coming down her cheek, "Isn't he wonderful?"

"Sorry, did I wake you?" coming back to herself. "Silly me, of course, I woke you up. I couldn't stop myself; I had to tell you."

. . .

"Ciccia, you know you can call me anytime. I just made coffee," I reply. "I am so happy for you; you look great."

"What's wrong? You look like shit," Gabrielle says worried.

"Grazie tante, Ciccia!"

"No ... you know what I mean," she continues, "you look like you have been crying."

"You know I don't do tears," I answer quickly. Shit, I didn't realise. "I am just tired, babe. I have just come back from mum's. Probably jet lag!"

"Jet lag from Napoli to London? Behave!"

"Well, maybe I am just getting old," trying to change the subject quickly. I don't want to ruin her moment. "Tell me everything. Will I have to curtsy when I see you next, Viscontessa?"

"Don't you dare ... I still can't believe it!"

"I am soo happy for you, Ciccia. You deserve it."

"Thank you," she replies. Then she comes closer to the screen, squinting, and looks deeply into my eyes, searching for answers.

. . .

"What?" I pause, holding my breath, "I am OK, really."

"We need a good catch-up next week when we return to London."

"Oh, is it 'we' already, uh?"

"No, no, yes ... oh shut up!"

"I am kidding, Ciccia."

"We are getting married in the new year, in Ireland. In his castle. *Incroyable, non?*" She looks so excited, like a kid at Christmas. "You are the maid of honour ... Pardon, matron of honour."

"I wouldn't miss it." That is so near ...

She adds, "Tom is going to ask Martin to be his best man." Are they that close? "How's Martin?" probing, pressing.

"Asleep," I reply.

"You know what I mean."

. . .

"I know. Martin is Martin."

"Babe..."

"I can't wait to see you again next week, Ciccia."

"Me too. See you soon. Bye."

"Bye."

The dull ache in my chest surges as the call with Gabrielle concludes, the weight of my secret pressing down on me with renewed force. I lean against the kitchen counter, my breathing erratic, as memories of time with Marco inundate my mind—our stolen moments in Italy. Marco is so much like my father—larger than life, commanding attention, and oh-so dangerous.

But it is all a temporary escape from the reality of life. I know that. My eyes drift to my left hand, where a simple gold wedding band mocks me. I remember when I exchanged vows with Martin ten years ago. The man I've married is still there, still the same: the reserved façade, a caring, sweet English gentleman, now a doting husband, father and son. Martin, my one constant in a sea of turmoil.

How have we drifted so far apart? How have I drifted so far?

IT ONLY TAKES ONE YES
PAOLA

The clink of wine glasses and chatter of well-heeled patrons fill Savini, the restaurant once the drawing room of the international belle époque. I settle into my seat, smoothing my pencil skirt. My eyes wander the white-clothed tables until they land on a familiar face—Marco, looking as devastatingly handsome as he did in our university days.

"Paola, che sorpresa!" Marco says, flashing a dazzling smile as he greets me and kisses my cheeks, "Time has stopped for you. Sei Bella come sempre."

"You haven't changed a bit either," I reply, taking in his impeccably tailored suit, salt-and-pepper hair and smooth-tanned skin. Same mischievous twinkle in his eye. "Do you still live in Napoli?"

"Si, Napoli è casa. Are you still dazzling the business world?" he asks, eyeing my corporate attire. "What brings you to Milan?" he continues, "besides destiny conspiring for us to meet again."

I try to ignore the flutter his words stir in me, but I chuckle like a little girl. "Just a quick work trip. My flight leaves tomorrow morning."

"Perfect, we have time," he says, flashing a dazzling smile. "Come and join me," he indicates at his table.

We catch up over Barolo and un risotto allo zafferano. The years melt away, and the old chemistry crackles between us like electricity. Marco is as charismatic and flirtatious as I remember, his hand now grazing my arm—so different from Martin's cool British reserve.

"I've thought about you over the years, you know," Marco confesses, pinning me with his intense dark eyes. "The one that got away."

That's not how I remember it ... "Marco... I'm married now," and I raise my left hand, the wedding band glinting under the lights of the Galleria. But as I say the words, desire spreads deep in my core. His hand finds my knee under the table, boldly sliding up my thigh.

"Cara, what happens in Milan stays in Milan," he reassures me with a cheeky wink. I should stop his hand and pull it away. But God help me, I don't want to. His touch ignites something dormant in me - an illicit thrill, an escape. One night to feel alive again...

And just like that, rational thought deserts me. I open my legs a little. Marco's fingers inch higher, grazing the lace edge of my underwear. I'm breathless, aching, the boredom of my safe, passionless marriage dissolving under his impudent touch. This is so wrong, but it feels so right.

I think of Martin back home in London; when was the last time he looked at me with raw hunger like Marco is now, like he couldn't wait to consume me?

"Don't overthink, Bella," Marco purrs, sensing my hesitation. "Scratch the hitch we never did. This is just a little fun between old friends. Nothing more. No one has to know." His fingers slip past my underwear, boldly stroking me. "Just one time."

Just, just … just …

A moan escapes my lips, my body betraying me. Just one night. A stolen moment out of time. It's not love, just sex - primal, therapeutic, like pressing a reset button. Surely a quick fling couldn't jeopardise everything I've built back home...could it?

Just …

· · ·

Marco settles the bill and rises, pulling me to my feet. "Let's get out of here." His eyes shine with promise, and I'm powerless to resist, even as a twinge of guilt niggles at my conscience.

The air caresses my flushed skin as we exit the restaurant. Marco's arm slung low around my waist, staking his claim. Anticipation and trepidation in my stomach, warring with the pulse of arousal between my legs as he hails a taxi.

What am I doing? Oh God, I can't remember; have I shaved?

No turning back now. As I slide into the backseat beside him, I silence the voice of reason, giving myself over to sensation and sin. For one reckless night, I want to feel something again, even if I hate myself in the morning. The taxi speeds through the lamp-lit streets, a blur of ancient architecture and modern store-fronts. Marco's hand rests possessively on my thigh, his thumb drawing maddening circles that make me squirm. I stare out the window, avoiding his penetrating gaze. If I look at him, I'll be lost. But I can feel the weight of his stare, undressing me, setting me on fire.

"Paola." His voice is as seductive as he is. "Look at me."

Exhaling, I turn. His scorching espresso eyes see straight into me, peeling back the layers of propriety. I am starved for passion, aching for it, and he knows it.

. . .

"I am going to fuck you so hard," he vows huskily, cupping my cheek. "I'm going to ruin you for your sissy English husband. You are going to come back and beg me for more."

"Don't ...talk ...about ... Mar-t" but I can't continue as his lips touch mine, not quite a kiss, his warm breath mingling with mine—self-preservation and decency battling with raw need.

"Don't speak," he orders. God, he smells good. Crisp and citrusy and achingly familiar - Acqua di Gio. Martin wears the same cologne, but it smells different on Marco. Forbidden. Intoxicating.

I wet my lips, pulse hammering in my throat. "Marco, I-" His fingers sink into my hair as he angles my head and silences me with a deep, long kiss, laying claim to my mouth with lips, teeth and tongue. I moan into the kiss, my treacherous body melting against his, surrendering to his dominance as the taxi flies through the city.

PACKING AND UNPACKING
PAOLA

Time has gone by so quickly. The wedding is this weekend, and we are getting ready to go. I fold Martin's button-down shirt, the soft blue fabric cool beneath my fingers, and carefully place it in his suitcase. The girls' chatter and laughter drift in from down the hall.

"Did you pack the girls' dresses?" Martin asks, his voice even, his eyes fixed on the task.

"Yes, they're in the garment bag." I gesture towards the door, where the bag hangs, the ruffled skirts of the flower girl dresses peeking out.

He nods, a small, tight smile on his lips. "Good. They're so excited."

· · ·

"A wedding in a castle in the Irish countryside, with a real Viscount; what little girl wouldn't be thrilled?" I say, trying to match his light tone, but the words feel hollow. I watch him arrange his ties, and I can't help but admire the quiet strength he exudes. I remember the first time we met. I was struck by his subtle, almost elusive handsomeness, which grows more evident the longer you look—the strong jaw, with a certain ruggedness, the English fair complexion that flushes so quickly, and the sandy brown hair neatly trimmed that catches the light as he moves. The glasses perched on his nose lend him an air of refined intellect, but it's his eyes—those steady blue-grey eyes— that truly captivated me. And his reserved, controlled composure from old times gone. The long walks, the endless chats, the courting. I wanted him to kiss me so badly, and I waited. And then I waited some more and waited and waited ... until I couldn't anymore and made the first move.

Not Marco, a philandering scoundrel incapable of showing any affection, a peacock demanding attention, possessive, who fucks me hard, makes me beg and then forgets about me until the next time. And he knows there is always a next time. The stolen moments, the guilt twisting my gut, yet I go back for more, begging.

"This Marco of yours," says Gabrielle, biting into her pappardelle with beef shin ragu, a Trullo's speciality. "He sounds pretty much like your father, *non*?" Gabrielle is the only one who knows my secret."Well, the way you described him anyway ... with your mother," she declares with her typical French directness. Her deep brown eyes staring, searching for a reaction. I don't like where this is going. "You told me you hated your father and your mother for forgiving him each time," she continues.

· · ·

Oh God, I want the floor to open and swallow me. "Where is the waiter?" I ask, trying to ignore what she said. "We need more wine." I stuff my mouth with a big handful of tagliarini with picked Dorset crab, Amalfi lemon, and chilli, hoping I can stall.

"We do. We need a lot more wine," she presses unperturbed. "Perhaps it will help you to talk about this." When we agreed to meet for lunch at Trullo, a lovely, tiny restaurant just around Highbury Corner on St. Paul's Road, I didn't imagine we would be talking about me.

"Today was supposed to be about you, your big adventure in New York, your reunion, the proposal ... You've just come back, tell me everything!" I say instead.

"Good try. You know the ending," she adds, lifting her left hand and moving her ring finger with the enormous engagement ring.

"I still can't get over how big it is," I say.

Gabrielle smiles like a cat with the cream. "Soo?? Aren't you going to answer?" Still pressing.

"I didn't hear a question ..." I reply, hoping it goes away.

Gabrielle looks at me pensively and says, "Marco is never going to give you what your father never could."

. . .

"Paola … love?" Martin's voice brings me back to reality, Gabrielle's voice still in my ears.

"Uh?"

"I think that's everything," he says, zipping up one suitcase with a decisive tug. He looks up at me, his expression unreadable. "Are you OK?"

"Yes, yes," I rush to answer. How could I have risked this? This life we've built, this family we've created? I want to say something to bridge the gap that seems to widen with each passing day, but the words stick in my throat. I nod, not trusting my voice. I zip up my case, the sound harsh in the quiet room.

"*La differenza mia cara,* for me it's just sex. I tell Marco I'm going over; if he is available, we meet; if he isn't, it is still OK, like a 'human vibrator' on call. Nothing else. He knows how to make me come, and he does his job. He doesn't want or need anything more from me and me from him". Just sex … Means nothing … I can't believe I said that to Gabrielle, like I felt nothing.

"Girls! Time to go!" Martin calls out, breaking the spell. He grabs both suitcases and heads for the door, his steps measured and sure.

I follow, trying to control my rising emotions. As we step into the hallway, I plaster on a smile, determined to make it through

346 | LAURA (L.A.) MARIANI

this weekend, one way or another. "Suck it up, Paola," I say to myself, "This is Gabri's and Tom's weekend."

My mind drifts back and forward to the memories I've tried so hard to bury. "Is it true? Am I still looking for his validation?" My father, with his charming smile and wandering eye, always ready with a compliment or a wink for any pretty woman who crossed his path. My mother, silent and stoic, her pain evident in the tightness around her eyes and the set of her jaw. The long nights I'd lie awake, listening to her muffled sobs, waiting for him to come back home from his latest floozy. The mornings after, the heavy silence at the breakfast table, the forced smiles and false cheer. "Is this what I've become?" A woman so desperate for love and validation that I'd risk everything I hold dear?

The drive to the airport is a blur, the chatter of our daughters fading into background noise as I grapple with the weight of my choices. Martin is quiet, absorbed in his thoughts. I want to reach out to him and take his hand in mine, but I can't bring myself to bridge the distance. At the airport, we go through the motions of checking in and shepherding our excited girls through security. They marvel at the planes and bustling crowds, their eyes wide with wonder. I feel a twinge of longing for that innocence. We board the plane and settle into our seats, Martin by the window, me in the middle, and our daughters in the aisle. I feel the weight of my secret pressing down on me. I glance at him, admiring the strong jawline and the silver starting to thread through his sandy hair.

I know my betrayal will shatter him. The thought of losing him, of losing this life we've built together, fills me with terror. The plane takes off. I close my eyes, trying to steady my breathing. "I have to find a way to make things right." I've spent my whole life determined to build a different life, to be different from my mother. "Have I become my father?"

Martin reaches over, his hand finding mine, his touch gentle and reassuring. "Everything alright, love?" he asks, his voice soft, his eyes searching mine.

I force a smile, squeezing his hand. "Just tired," I lie, the words tasting bitter. "It's been a busy week getting ready for the trip."

He nods. "It'll be good to get away for a bit." Martin chuckles a warm, rich sound that usually comforts me but now only amplifies my guilt and shame. He deserves so much better than this. So much better than me. I close my eyes again, trying to block out the thoughts, but they come anyway, unsolicited, unwanted. Flashes of Marco, stolen moments, the thrill, the passion, the aching, the empty aftermath. The plane hums around us, and as I sit here with Martin's hand in mine, and our daughters' laughter in my ears, I feel like I'm on a knife's edge, waiting for the inevitable fall.

LIES, LIES, LIES …
MARTIN

P aola looks at me, clearing her throat. "I think that's everything then. Did you get the car arranged?"

I nod, still not meeting her eyes. "It'll be here at noon."

"Good. Girls, do you have everything packed?" Paola calls out. "We leave for the airport in two hours!" Her dark hair falls in glossy waves around her olive-toned face, eyes flashing with a barely-contained intensity as she glances over. Excited giggles and hurried footsteps sound from down the hall.

"Yes, Ma! Almost done!" Paola smiles.

The girls' exuberance is infectious, even if her enthusiasm feels forced. Silence stretches between us. Paola busies herself with the luggage tags, seemingly unaware of the chasm that has cracked open in our marriage.

. . .

"Paola, honey? Your phone is buzzing .... Paola?" She is in the shower, her phone lighting up on the nightstand... I click on the message preview before I can stop and take a peak. My heart pounding.

> "You were a very good girl last night... You were a dirty little slut, you like it when I fuck you hard ..."

The shock is visceral, a gut-wrenching realisation that the woman I love, the mother of my children, has been unfaithful. The name on the screen makes my blood run cold: Marco. The phone clatters from my hand onto the bed, my head spinning, bile rising in my throat. All those trips to Italy, those visits to her sick mother -- how could I have been so blind? The signs were all there. Her distracted air, her renewed passion that felt out of place...

I squeeze my eyes shut against the onslaught of emotions. Sadness, betrayal, and anger crash over me in waves, stealing my breath. How could she do this? To me, to our family? After all these years...

The bathroom door opens, and I hastily replace the phone, arranging my features into a neutral mask. I can't confront her, not now, not with this anger inside, not with the girls nearby. I need time to think and process.

. . .

"Martin?" Paola's voice cut through the painful trance. "The car will be here soon. We should get the bags downstairs."

I jolt, swallow hard, and reach for the suitcases. Even now, the wounds are still raw. "Right. I'll take these down." My voice sounds hollow to my own ears. Paola watches me go, her confident exterior cracking for just a moment. Regret flickers across her face, mingled with something akin to longing. But she straightens her shoulders and follows me out, moving in stubborn silence as the distance between us widens.

I still remember every moment and detail of when I first saw her. It was a warm, sun-drenched afternoon in Rome nearly twelve years ago. I was attending a conference in the Eternal City when I spotted her across a crowded piazza. She was laughing with friends, her dark hair cascading in glossy waves, and her olive skin glowing under the sun.

"My God, she's gorgeous," I was transfixed, my heart pounding in a way I'd never experienced before. I just wanted to go over and claim her as mine. I fell hard and fast, desire cursing through my veins, a surge of unbridled possessiveness. It took me nearly an hour to compose myself enough to approach her. I had to control myself. The spectre of my father's abuse and my mother's suffering had left me wary of my own emotions. I feared the intensity of my feelings for Paola, worried I might somehow become the man I despised.

"Paola is having an affair," I blurted out, "Well, regular sex with someone, to be specific ... she is a very passionate woman, " I continued, justifying. "I've never been inclined that way," lies I told myself. "All I ever wanted was a companion and a family. She is an amazing mother and a good wife. We have a great life: she has her career, and I have my family. And I would never leave my girls."

"And you are OK with that?" Tom asked me with a disbelieving look.

"Not exactly, but I have learnt to live with it. She is careful."
    "Learnt to live with it?" more lies. I've shied away from the raw, unbridled desire I crave. That she craves.

"She is a flesh and blood woman with her faults and failures. Flesh and blood, my friend. And you have put her on a pedestal, idolised her. You can't make passionate love to someone you are afraid to break; even I know that". I said that to Tom about Gabrielle. Yes, I- SAID-THAT!

"Have I failed her to be the man she needs? Have I failed me?" The thought lodges like a splinter in my heart. We have built a life together, a family. But the cracks are showing now, the foundation of our marriage straining under the weight of unspoken truths and unfulfilled desires. Mine.

Paola emerges from the house, our daughters in tow. We begin our journey, the lush English countryside giving way to the promise of Ireland's emerald hills.

"You were a very good girl last night..."

That text plays over and over in my head. "Why didn't I confront her?" I rationalised my decision, telling myself that I couldn't tear our family apart, that our daughters needed both parents and that I could somehow find a way to ignore it and move forward. I watch Paola settle into the passenger seat beside me. The thought gnaws at me as the Uber drives through the countryside. The silence between us is thick.

Tom's and Gabrielle's love story plays out in his mind...

"Man, this is crazy. You can't go to New York and wait at the top of the Empire State Building without knowing if she will show up. I know New York is home for you, but still, it's crazy," I said. "It has been six months without contact."

"Have you told Paola you know about her and her Italian stud?" Tom replied.

My cheeks went red. "Touché."

"Gabrielle has everything she needs if she wants to come over and see me: plane ticket, hotel reservation. She just needs to be sure she still wants it. She still wants me, us".

His gamble paid off.

. . .

I glance at Paola, taking in the elegant lines of her profile. She is still the most beautiful woman I've ever seen, she makes my heart race and my soul ache. As we arrive at the airport, I brace myself for the journey ahead.

"This weekend belongs to Tom and Gabrielle." Viscount Thomas Darcy Vitale Fitzwilliam II, actually, "My problem can wait until Monday."

The road ahead would be difficult, a battle, but I am finally ready to wage it, no matter the cost.

ROSINGS PARK

PAOLA

The stately manor house rises before us, a limestone Georgian beauty nestled amongst emerald green hills that roll endlessly to the horizon. Tom's ancestral estate, recently inherited after the truth of his noble lineage came to light. I take it all in—the ornate wrought iron gate, the manicured hedges lining the gravel drive, the marble fountain tinkling melodically in the courtyard. It's like stepping into the pages of an Austen novel—breathtaking, romantic, idyllic—everything Gabrielle deserves for her wedding.

"Welcome to Rosings Park," Tom greets us with a broad smile, one arm wrapped around Gabrielle's waist. She looks radiant, at home in her new role as lady of the manor.

Martin reaches for my hand as we ascend the limestone steps, but I slip mine free to hug Gabrielle instead, pasting on a smile. "It's gorgeous, Gabri. It's like a fairy tale! I'm so happy for you." My words sound brittle to my own ears. I avoid Martin's eyes.

. . .

I inhale deeply, the fresh and clean air tinged with the scent of salt off the nearby sea. Tom clasps Martin's shoulder, his grin wide and welcoming. "Martin, Paola! Let me introduce you to the family."

He guides us into a grand foyer, all marble and gilt, where a small gathering awaits. Tom's brothers, as tall and striking as he is, flank an elegant elderly woman in a velvet armchair. Gabrielle's parents are nearby, her mother's curious gaze sweeping over me.

"Everyone, this is Paola, Gabrielle's friend, her husband Martin, and their lovely girls, Sofia and Emilia." The girls smile shyly, overwhelmed by the opulent surroundings.

"Ah, Paola!" Tom's grandmother rises, taking my hands in her papery grip. "I've heard so much about you. And what a handsome couple you two make!"

If only she knew …

"Thank you, Lady Fitzwilliam. We're delighted to be here," I murmur.

Gabrielle's mother approaches, air-kissing my cheeks in the French fashion. "Paola, *comment vas-tu chérie?*" Her eyes, a piercing dark brown so like Gabrielle's, seem to penetrate my very soul.

. . .

"*Très bien, Madame.*" The pleasantries slip out naturally, even as my stomach twists with anxiety. I love Madame Arkin. Her gaze lingers on my face a beat too long, her lips pursing. She senses something amiss between Martin and me, but discretion prevents her from prying. For now.

"Come, let me show you to your rooms," Gabrielle interjects, rescuing me. "You must be exhausted from the trip."

Gratefully, I follow her up the sweeping staircase while Martin and the girls go wandering. As the door closes , I sink onto the plush four-poster bed, my head spinning. The opulent surroundings fade away as my mind churns. A soft knock at the door startles me. "Paola? Are you decent?" Gabrielle's voice, muffled by the heavy oak, is laced with concern.

"Come in," I call, straightening my shoulders and pasting on a smile.

She enters, her dark hair tumbling around her shoulders. "Is everything alright, *chérie*? You seemed... tense earlier."

"I'm fine, just tired from the journey."

Gabrielle studies me, her head tilted. "Paola ... Did you two have a fight?"

. . .

My smile falters, and I look away, blinking back sudden tears. "No, no. I'm fine .... don't worry about me. This is your weekend."

She moves closer, resting a comforting hand on my arm. "*Chérie*, you'll get through it. You and Martin, you're meant to be together. Anyone can see that."

I nod, swallowing hard. "Thanks, Gabri." I hug her fiercely, drawing strength from her.

A chime sounds from somewhere within the house, signalling the start of the festivities. "That'll be the dressing gong," Gabrielle says, pulling back. "Mum's insisting on a formal dinner tonight to welcome everyone. Will you be alright?"

"Of course." I square my shoulders, determined to play my part. "Let me freshen up, and I'll be down shortly."

———

I take a deep breath, trying to steady my nerves as I make my way down the grand staircase. The sound of laughter and chatter drifts up from below, and I pause for a moment, my hand gripping the polished railing. Martin is waiting at the bottom, looking dashing in his tailored suit. But there's a distance in his eyes that wasn't there before, a coolness that sends a shiver down my spine. He offers me his arm, and I take it, forcing a smile.

· · ·

"You look beautiful," he murmurs, but the words feel hollow.

"Thank you." I smooth down the silk of my dress, feeling the weight of every eye in the room upon us as we enter the dining hall.

The table is set with gleaming silver and crystal, and the centrepieces are a riot of colourful blooms. Tom's grandmother, the Dowager Viscountess, presides at the head, her keen gaze missing nothing. "Paola, my dear," she says, beckoning me closer. "Come, sit by me."

I obey, grateful for the reprieve from Martin's presence.

Across the table, Gabrielle's mother catches my eye, her brow furrowed in concern. "Is everything alright, *chérie*?" she asks softly, her French accent lending a musical lilt to the words.

I force a bright smile, hoping it reaches my eyes. "Of course, Madame Arkin. Just a bit tired from the journey, that's all."

She looks unconvinced but lets the matter drop, turning to speak with her husband. I pick at my food.

The evening stretches on forever, each course more lavish than the last. By the time the plates are cleared, and the men retire to the library for brandy and cigars, I'm exhausted, my cheeks aching from the effort of maintaining a facade of cheerful serenity.

I make my excuses and slip away, seeking the solace of our bedroom. Martin chatting away with Tom and his brothers. The girl are in their room. I sink onto the edge of the bed, my head in my hands, and finally let the tears come, hot and bitter, against my skin.

I KNOW
MARTIN

The phone lights up in the dark with an incoming message. Paola moans and stretches, slowly pulling herself up from the bed.

Buz, buzzzz.

She reaches out and then stops. "Go on, take it," I say, "Take it," Paola looks terrified.

"Here," and I drop the phone on the bed, "Read it. ... Don't you want to know what your lover is doing?"

"What do you mean?"

"There's no point pretending anymore," my voice is wavering but eerily calm. "I know what you have done." The words are coming out, and I can't stop them. "Every time you went to Italy, I knew." My heart pounds against my ribcage. The room spins slightly, and I reach for a hand to steady myself.

"Martin, I..." Her voice cracks.

"Don't you dare deny it," I step closer, my jaw hurting. "Do you have any idea how much it killed me inside, Paola? Wondering what you were doing with him? The images torturing my mind? And you just went on lying to my face."

Tears spill down her cheeks. "I'm so sorry. I never meant to hurt you."

"Well, you did hurt me—you pulled me apart." My voice rises, echoing off the ancient walls, my hands balled into fists at my sides, my broad shoulders shaking.

She reaches out slowly to touch my arm, but for the first time, I flinch away as if burned. "Don't!" I warn through gritted teeth. "I'm trying so hard not to lose control right now ..."

I can't turn into Him. I won't.

"You're nothing like him," she whispers as if knowing. But the words sound hollow. Gabrielle and Tom's laughter drifts up from the courtyard below.

. . .

"Tell me how to fix this," she pleads. "I'll do anything. I love you, Martin."

Tears stream down my face, the anger finally gushing out. The stone walls seem to close in around us. The truth is finally out. She knows I know.

"Martin, I..." her voice cracks, the words catching in her throat. "Please, let me explain. It was a mistake, a terrible mistake. I was weak."

I can't believe she said that. "A mistake? You call months of lying and sneaking around a mistake?" My jaw clenches some more.

"I know I don't deserve your forgiveness, but I'm begging you, Martin. Please don't give up on us. I love you, and I'll do whatever it takes to make this right. " Her words are too much to bear. Doesn't she know?

"Give up on you? WTF, Paola!" the pain is now intolerable, "I fucking LOVE you! I fucking meant those vows ... For better, for worse ... in sickness and in health ... till death do us part. Those vows ... those vows were not just pretty words on a pretty day." My voice is strained, "I stood there and promised, knowing change will happen and still commit to being together ... till death DO US PART."

. . .

Paola's head snaps up, her eyes filled with disbelief and hope. "You love me, even after what I've done? Why didn't you say anything?"

"Why didn't I say anything? Why?" why didn't I? "Because I was waiting for you to stop. Because I wanted you to choose me, to want me, us, more." I move closer. "You are fucking mine, you belong to me." She is still wearing her tight red dress. I pull the straps down and grab her large breasts, squeezing her nipples. "These are mine!"

She looks at me then, really looks at me, and a long moan escapes her lips. I pull and squeeze some more before turning her over. I lift her dress and place my hand between her soft thighs, pulling at her lace underwear. "This pussy is mine."

"Martin," she quivers.

I back her down against the bed, pinning her with my body. I can smell her arousal over the faint scent of her perfume. I groan in her ear, "You're mine, Paola. Mine, do you hear me?"

"Yes, ..."

Her lace black undies are soaked, and I rip them off before sliding my fingers into her wet heat. "Oh, Martin," she moans, her back arching, her hips pressing against me. I press a finger into her slippery opening, then another, circling my thumb over her swollen clit, making her whimper and squirm under my touch. Her hands grip the edges of the bed, screaming.

"Do you like being claimed?" Her response is a loud cry, and I know she does. Anger replaced by an overwhelming desire to pound into her.

"No, no, please don't stop," she whines as I pull my fingers out.

"I'm going to fuck you all night," I growl, and I thrust deep into her, over and over. "Whose pussy is this?"

"Yours, y-ooou-rs ..."

My hands roam up and down her body, cupping and squeezing her breasts. I can feel myself nearing the edge.

"Come for me, baby." She screams my name over and over as I continue to pounce into her tightness, feeling it pulsing and tightening around me. Finally, she falls over the edge, and I let myself go too. I should have done this a long time ago.

THE BIG DAY
PAOLA

The morning light seeps through the thick curtains, casting a warm glow on the tangled sheets. Martin's arms are still wrapped tightly around me, his grip soothing and protective. I nestle deeper into his embrace, not wanting to leave this safe haven.

"Good morning," he whispers, softly kissing my hair.

I turn to face him, taking in his handsome face. The man I've always desired has been here all along, by my side. "Thank you," I whisper back, a smile spreading across my lips.

"Well, I was good," he chuckles, waggling his eyebrows mischievously. "Fucking awesome, actually..." We both burst into laughter. "I can always do a repeat performance now if you'd like." His voice is low and suggestive, his hardness pressed against me.

· · ·

"I'd love to," I reply breathlessly, my desire growing at his touch. "But we have to get ready for the big day. The girls will be knocking down the door any minute now."

Martin groans playfully, knowing that our duties call for us to rise now and start preparing. "Yes, the flower girls are beyond excited for their role. And their pretty flowy dresses." He grins, picturing our daughters' excitement and enthusiasm for the upcoming event. We reluctantly untangle ourselves from each other and start getting ready for the day ahead.

The bedroom door opens, "Mum, Dad," Emilia and Sofia burst in, their voices loud and full of excitement. Martin and I erupt into laughter, glad we stopped when we did.

"I'll jump in the shower first and then go to help Tom to get ready; I'll take my suit with me."

I nod. "I'll see you later."

"We'll meet at the altar again, Mrs Rossi-Wright," he says.

"Mrs Wright," I reply and nods smiling.

––––––––

The grandiose estate is adorned with swaths of white silk and arrangements of fragrant blossoms, all ready for the wedding. The scent of jasmine and gardenias hangs heavy in the air, mingling with the delicious aromas wafting from the adjacent feasting hall. The sun glows over the manicured gardens, bathing the scene in a warm, ethereal light. The guests are all adorned in their finest attire, fit for the occasion.

Sofia and Emilia walk down the aisle, gently tossing rose petals. "They look so happy, I am so proud". Gabrielle walks behind them on her father's arm, wearing a breathtaking ivory gown with lace appliqués and a sweeping train. I can see her eyes sparkle as she sees Tom waiting for her at the altar, looking tall and handsome in his tuxedo. I stand by Gabrielle's side as her matron of honour while Martin is beside Tom as his best man, looking ever so dapper in his suit.

The scent of fresh flowers fills the air. The family chaplain begins the ceremony, his voice steady and warm. As Tom begins reciting his vows first, I catch Martin's eye and see him silently mouthing the words along with Tom. My own throat tightens: "In sickness and in health...for richer and for poor...till death do us part."

I can feel tears filling up my eyes. I can't cry, I can't cry ...

As Gabrielle takes her turn, I move my lips along with her: "In sickness and in health...for richer and for poor...till death do us part."

After the ceremony, the wedding party moves to the sumptuous feast on long banquet tables adorned with silverware and crystal glasses. Servants circulate the room, refilling glasses with the finest wines and liquors. After the meal, the orchestra plays a lively waltz as the newlyweds dance their first dance, followed by the traditional father-daughter dance.

"Mrs Wright, may I have this dance?"

"With pleasure, Mr Wright."

Martin leads me on the dance floor, his hands firm on my body, pulling me close, claiming me once more, gently kissing my forehead. I sigh into the kiss, my arms wrapping around his neck like I fear he'd disappear. Martin's hand trails up and down my hips while he kisses down my jawline, his tongue flicking my sensitive spot.

"Martin," I moan, my nails digging into his back.

He breathes against my skin, "I love you, Paola," his voice deep with emotion and desire.

"I love you too, Martin." With that, he claims my lips. The room is filled with laughter and heavy breathing, but the most important sound of all is the sound of our hearts now beating in sync.

EPILOGUE

D ing dong ... Ding dong ... Ding ...Dong.

Sunlight streams through the vibrant stained glass windows, radiating a kaleidoscope of colours across the Church's ancient stone walls. Gabrielle and Tom are beaming with pride as they cradle their precious bundle, their faces shining with the love and wonder of new parenthood. The Church is full, and the soft murmur of loved ones gathered to celebrate the occasion fills the air.

Martin leans close to my ear and whispers, "It will be us ... soon." His hand finds the slight swell of my belly, a secret we've yet to share with the world. I glance at Martin, taking in the confident set of his shoulders and squeeze his hand, my heart full of love and gratitude. My man. My husband.

. . .

The priest begins the ceremony. Gabrielle and Tom approach the baptismal font with their newborn daughter in their arms.

He then calls us forward, "Paola, Martin, Are you ready to help the parents of this child in their duty as Christian parents?" Snif snif. Gabri's mother is sobbing with joy.

"We do," we answer in unison, our voices strong and clear.

"Is it your will that Anne Shobhan Vitale Fitzwilliam should be baptised in the faith of the Church, which we have all professed with you? "

"It is."

"Anne Shobhan, I baptise you in the name of the Father," He says, pouring water on her forehead, "and of the Son," pouring water upon her a second time, "and of the Holy Spirit."

As we exit the Church, Martin pulls me close, his lips brushing against my temple, his hand possessively firm on my back. I tilt my face up to his and return the kiss. A boyish grin spreads across his face. "How are you feeling, love?" he murmurs, his breath warm against my ear, and pulls me into his strong embrace, his hand resting protectively on the gentle swell of my belly. I feel a rush of desire.

.   .   .

"Perfect," I whisper back, leaning into his touch. "Absolutely perfect."

QUOTE

" Marriage is the school of love where change is inevitable. You can choose whether you grow together or apart."
- Fr . Mike Schmitz
(Sunday homily 29 October 2021)

GET YOUR FREE EBOOK

Sign up the Laura (L.A.) Mariani mailing list for a FREE steamy romance.

You'll be the first to hear about new releases, exclusive offers, bonus content and all Laura's news. You can even email her back. She loves chatting with her readers!

To claim your free ebook visit:
https://laura-mariani-author.ck.page/freeshortstory

AUTHOR'S NOTE

Thank you so much for reading **The Nine Lives of Gabrielle.**

I hope you enjoyed the stories as a form of escapism, but perhaps you also glimpsed something beneath as you read. A review would be much appreciated as it helps other readers discover the story.

Thanks.

Places in the book

I have set the story in real places in London, my beloved Islington, New York, Paris and Milan.

You can see some of the places/mentions below - find out more about them or perhaps, go and visit:

London

- Balthazar, London
- Belgravia

- British Gand Prix/Silverstone
- Camden Passage
- Canonbury Square and Gardens
- Covent Garden
- Highbury & Islington
- Islington Farmers Market
- Le Boudin Blanc
- London Borough of Richmond
- NoMad London
- One New Change
- Royal Opera House, London
- Salut
- St Paul's Cathedral
- The Alwyne Castle
- The Estorick Collection of Modern Art
- The Mandarin Oriental Hotel
- The Twenty Two
- Trullo.
- 2 Veneti
- Wimbledon - The Championship

Milan

- Galleria Vittorio Emanuele II
- Savini

New York

- Balthazar, New York
- Blue Bottle Coffee
- Central Park
- Empire State Building
- Magnolia Bakery
- NYC West Village
- Rockefeller Center

- The Langham, New York, Fifth Avenue
- The Metropolitan Opera, New York
- The New York Public Library
- The Shinnecock Golf Club
- The Statue of Liberty
- Times Square
- TownePlace Suites, Manhattan / Times Square

Paris

- Bois de Vincennes
- Bois de Boulogne,
- Buttes-Chaumont
- Cinema en Plein Air festival
- Eurostar
- Gare du Nord
- Jardin du Luxembourg
- Jardins des Plantes
- Le Metro
- Parc Rives de Seine
- Paris Plages
- Parc Floral
- Parc de la Villette Palais-Royal
- Parc Monceau
- Parc Montsouris
- TGV (train à grande vitesse)
- Tour Eiffel
- Tour Montparnasse

Bibliography

I read different books as part of my research. Some of them together with other references include:

A Theory of Human Motivation - **Abraham Maslow**

Psycho-Cybernetics - **Maxwell Maltz**
Self Mastery Through Conscious Autosuggestion - **Émile Coué**
The Artist Way - **Julia Cameron**.
The Complete Reader - **Neville Goddard**, compiled and edited
by **David Allen**
Tools of Titans - **Tim Ferris**

An Affair to Remember is a 1957 American romance film directed
by Leo McCarey and starring Cary Grant and Deborah Kerr. It
the story of two people in love who agree to reunite at the top of
the Empire State Building in six months' time if they succeeded
in ending their current relationships and starting new careers.
On the day of their rendezvous however, whilst hurrying to
reach the place of the encounter, the woman is struck down by a
car while crossing a street and is gravely injured. Meanwhile, he
is waiting for her unaware of the accident. After many hours
waiting, he leaves believing that she has rejected him.
They reunite, of course, at the end of the movie.

The **"Bermondsey Goes Balearic"** article in the late 1987 by Paul
Oakenfold for Terry Farley and Pete Heller's Boys Own fanzine
(*it's all gone Pete Tong*).

Law and Order : Criminal Intent - American crime
drama television, third series in Dick Wolf's successful Law and
Order franchise. Detective Robert Goren is one of the main
original character played by actor Vincent D'Onofrio, a modern
tortured but brilliant Sherlock Holmes like figure.

Madame Butterfly is an opera in three acts by Giacomo Puccini,
with an Italian libretto by Luigi Illica and Giuseppe Giacosa,
premiered at La Scala, in Milan in 1904.

Midsomer Murders - British crime drama television series
adapted from the novels in the *Chief Inspector Barnaby* book series

(created by Caroline Graham). The series focuses on various murder cases that take place within small country villages across the fictional English county of Midsomer.

Keeping up Appearances - British sitcom starring Patricia Routledge as the eccentric snob Hyacinth Bucket. It broadcast from 1990 to 1995.

The Vicar of Dibley - British sitcom starring Dawn French as the Vicar of the rural parish of Dibley, It made its debut in 1994.

ABOUT THE AUTHOR

Laura Alexandra (L.A.) Mariani is a best selling author of Short & Steamy Romance | Where Alpha Males Meet Fierce Heroines for Sweet Endings, your go-to author for captivating romance tales that will sweep you off your feet and keep you on the edge of your seat!

When Laura is not weaving stories of love, desire and suspense, you'll find her exploring the vibrant streets of London, drawing inspiration from its hidden corners and bustling markets, or strolling through the charming streets of Paris, savoring street food in Rome, or relaxing on a sun-kissed beach in Bali, her journeys fuelling her creativity and infuse her stories with wanderlust.

You can also follow her on

Printed in Great Britain
by Amazon